DREAMS

OF

SIGNIFICANT

GIRLS

Also by Cristina Garcia

I Wanna Be Your Shoebox

DREAMS

OF

SIGNIFICANT

GIRLS

CRISTINA GARCÍA

SIMON & SCHUSTER BFYR

New York London Toronto Sydney New Delhi

An imprint of Simon & Schuster Children's Publishing Division
1230 Avenue of the Americas, New York, New York 10020

SIMON & SCHUSTER BFYR is a trademark of Simon & Schuster, Inc.
For information about special discounts for bulk purchases, please contact
Simon & Schuster Special Sales at 1-866-506-1949 or
business@simonandschuster.com.
The Simon & Schuster Speakers Bureau can bring authors to your live event.
For more information or to book an event, contact the Simon & Schuster
Speakers Bureau at 1-866-248-3049 or visit our website at
www.simonspeakers.com.
Also available in a SIMON & SCHUSTER BFYR hardcover edition
Book design by Krista Vossen
The text for this book is set in Andrade Regular.
Manufactured in the United States of America
First SIMON & SCHUSTER BFYR paperback edition May 2012
2 4 6 8 10 9 7 5 3 1
The Library of Congress has cataloged the hardcover edition as follows:
García, Cristina, 1958–
Dreams of significant girls / Cristina García. — 1st ed.
p. cm.
Summary: In the 1970s, a teenaged Iranian princess, a German-Canadian girl,
and a Cuban-Jewish girl from New York City become friends when they spend
three summers at a Swiss boarding school.
ISBN 978-1-4169-7920-3 (hardcover)
[1. Friendship—Fiction. 2. Summer—Fiction. 3. Boarding schools—Fiction.
4. Schools—Fiction. 5. Switzerland—History—20th century—Fiction.] I. Title.
PZ7.G155624Dr 2011
[Fic]—dc22
2010002585
ISBN 978-1-4169-7930-2 (pbk)
ISBN 978-1-4169-8587-7 (eBook)

For my daughter, Pilar

Acknowledgments

Special thanks to Samantha Lewin

Little poppies, little hell flames,
Do you do no harm?

—Sylvia Plath

DREAMS

OF

SIGNIFICANT

GIRLS

BOOK ONE:

THE ACCIDENTAL ART OF HYPNOSIS

SUMMER 1971

DAY
ONE

VIVIEN WAHL

Sometimes I think my parents sent me to Switzerland because
they didn't want me around. Things were going downhill for
my father ever since we moved from Miami to New York City.
My dad was kind of unusual for a Cuban exile. First, he was
Jewish when most Cubans were Catholic, like my mother.
Second, he was politically liberal—a registered Democrat, in
fact—and believed that Cubans *off* the island should talk to the
Cubans *on* the island. That made him Public Enemy Number
One in Miami.

When the other Cuban exiles found out that Max Wahl had
gone to Havana to hold secret meetings with El Líder, they
called him a traitor, and worse. We got threatening phone calls
in the middle of the night and we had to check for bombs under
our car—a 1957 Cadillac, identical to our old car in Havana. Papi

learned how to shoot a gun, kept one in a holster under his jacket. He took me to shooting ranges behind my mother's back. Kids at school shunned me, called me the Communist's daughter. Nobody invited me to their birthday parties. Plus people boycotted my father's three jewelry stores and he had to close down two of them in a year.

My mother begged my father to leave Miami, to start fresh in another city where no one would ostracize him for his political beliefs. So when I was twelve years old, we moved to New York City. Talk about shock. Talk about noise. Talk about rude. But it didn't take me more than a month to get used to it, and to love it. Everyone was curious about me. They wanted to know why I spoke Spanish and whether I'd ever seen an alligator. When I told my classmates that I'd been to the Everglades and had gotten *this close* to an alligator—showing them pictures to prove it—I was instantly popular.

Things didn't go as well for my parents. Papi worked all the time. He traveled to Africa to buy diamonds for his new import business. We hardly ever saw him. This made my mother very lonely. Whenever I wanted to hang out with friends after school, she made me feel so guilty that half the time I didn't go. Late at night, I'd hear my parents arguing. Mom cried and accused Dad of abandoning her. She suspected that he was having an affair. He countered that maybe he didn't want to come home to a depressed wife every night. So off I went to "safe" Switzerland so they could sort things out.

I'd never been on a flight by myself before, much less one where you got to choose what you wanted to eat from a menu. I ordered everything that came with cream sauce and a crème brûlée for dessert. Then I settled in to read my volume of J. D. Salinger stories. I brought ten books with me, all fiction. The Swiss camp promised that I'd be exceedingly busy: three hours of French classes in the morning, sports and activities in the afternoon (I chose horseback riding, water skiing, cooking, and ceramics), with nightly activities on top of that. I packed a flashlight in case my only time to read was under the bedcovers. In third grade, I got glasses from reading in the dark. Every time my mother looked at me with my thick tortoiseshell glasses, she'd sigh, as if I'd been permanently disfigured.

The plane flew only half the night but because of the time change, it was already morning when we arrived in Geneva. The Pierpont Boarding School for Girls had a booth set up in the airport to greet the students, who came from around the world. On the shuttle bus to campus, I talked to a girl from Turkey and another from Sweden and heard languages I couldn't figure out at all. There was a sense of nervous excitement, as if we'd eaten too much chocolate. Almost everyone spoke a little English, and that quickly became the common language. There was a shy girl from Italy who couldn't join the conversation, so I tried to translate as best I could.

We drove along the shores of Lake Geneva for a while before coming to the village of Rolle. The first thing I noticed were the number of pastry shops everywhere. They looked perfect, with éclairs and petit fours beckoning to me from the glistening windows. Let me just tell this straight: I have a serious sweet tooth. I believe every meal should start with dessert and work its way backward. Don't even bother with appetizers. I was a pretty decent baker and made everything from scratch: vanilla chip macadamia cookies, double fudge cake, you name it. I was desperate to go to cooking school but my parents told me it wasn't a career fit for an educated girl.

When the bus turned into the majestic, oak-lined driveway of Pierpont, everyone stopped talking for a minute. It was a sunny day and the grounds were impeccable: rose gardens and elephant topiaries and arched trellises with purple bell-shaped flowers I'd never seen before. It was like entering paradise. During the year, Pierpont was one of the fanciest boarding schools in Europe. But in the summer, it opened its doors for a month and became a kind of luxury camp for kids who wanted, or who were forced by their parents, to study French.

I looked around and wondered if the other students thought it as beautiful as I did. Maybe they were so wealthy that nothing impressed them. I started thinking about my father and how he'd lost so much money in Miami and now had to go flying off to Africa to make a living; about our rambling apartment on West Sixty-fifth Street; about my mother shopping the sales at Lord & Taylor. We were still well off but probably nothing like the girls who came here.

By the time I got to my room, one of my roommates had already claimed the bed by the window. Her name was Ingrid and she was Canadian-German and alarmingly tall. I had to strain my neck to talk to her. She wore a gigantic mood ring on her left middle finger that was indicating extreme hostility. Frankly, the German part of her made me kind of nervous after all the World War II stories I'd heard from my dad. I calmed down by telling myself that this girl had nothing to do with what'd happened to Papi thirty years ago.

Ingrid was fifteen, a year older than me, but she seemed a lot older; not just because of her height but because of the way she carried herself, as if she knew about everything in advance. She had this enormous toolbox beside her bed but I was afraid to ask her what was in it. I couldn't imagine why anyone would need a wrench in this place. The first thing Ingrid did was offer me a cigarette, even though the teachers had told us during orientation that smoking was forbidden except for the senior girls, who had their own smoking lounge.

I took one, trying to look like I knew what I was doing. She pulled out a gold lighter with the initials *I. B.* and I held my cigarette to the flame.

"You might want to try putting the cigarette in your mouth," Ingrid said with a smirk.

I shrugged then sucked on the end of that cigarette for all it was worth. My mouth and nose filled with hot smoke but it also felt like it was going behind my eyes, out my ears. At that rate, the fire department would be arriving any minute. Predictably, I had a coughing fit. Ingrid ignored this fact and pulled out some miniature bottles of liquor she'd saved from the airplane and offered to make us a welcome drink.

"Maybe later," I croaked. I had the feeling she was trying to test me, to see how far I would go. She drank down the contents of a red labeled bottle of whiskey in one gulp.

"Have you ever worn a paper dress?" she asked flippantly.

"Uh, no."

"I highly recommend them. They save time undressing, if you know what I mean."

Thankfully, the dinner bell broke up the awkwardness

and we headed down to the dining room. There were place cards at every table and we scrambled to find our seats. After interminable announcements in French, we got down to the business of eating. On a culinary basis alone, I knew I was going to like it at Pierpont. Never mind the steamed artichokes with garlic remoulade. Or the grilled pork chops with roasted potatoes. For dessert, there was a delicious apple tart topped with crème anglaise.

Between mouthfuls I chatted with a pint-size New Yorker named Hope, who informed me immediately that she lived on Park Avenue and Sixty-fifth. When I told her that I lived on Sixty-fifth Street too, but on the west side *and* I went to public school, she sniffed and turned her attention to the neighbor on her left. To my right was a tentative Egyptian girl who spoke perfect, British-accented English. Jamila was tiny and fine boned, like a hummingbird. She couldn't have weighed more than eighty pounds soaking wet. We found common ground in books. Jamila was a huge fan of E. M. Forster—a writer I'd heard of but hadn't yet read—as well as Virginia Woolf. Definitely more advanced than me but we agreed to exchange books over the summer. I was relieved to have made a friend.

After dinner, we listened to the extracurricular instructors deliver presentations about their classes. The waterskiing coach went off on some long digression about Descartes. A Dutch girl who'd been there the year before explained that the coach was getting a doctorate in philosophy at the Sorbonne. The cooking teacher, Monsieur d'Aubigné, gave his spiel dressed in kitchen whites and a toque, slapping a wooden spoon in one hand. The most hilarious pitch came from the water ballet instructor, Madame Delfin (that was her real name, I swear), who began demonstrating underwater breathing techniques right on the spot. When everyone laughed, she furiously gasped like a flounder.

Back in my room, our third and last roommate—cinnamon skinned with enormous brown eyes—was settling herself on the bed nearest the door. She didn't look too happy about it. I introduced myself and tried to ask her a few neutral questions. She replied with minimal syllables, as if each word were painful to utter.

"So what's your name?"

"Shirin."

"Where are you from?"

"Iran."

"What do you like to do?"

"Mathematics."

"Mathematics?"

"Yes."

"Really?"

"Yes."

Okay, so maybe this roommate thing wasn't going to work out too well, after all.

SHIRIN FIROUZ

Despite the inconveniences, I was willing to try to get along. My three older brothers had gone to boarding school in Switzerland and were established at good colleges, or in the military. (Bahman was studying chemistry at Oxford; Asad was finishing his engineering degree at Heidelberg; and Cyrus had joined the Air Force and was flying fighter jets.) I was the youngest in my family by nine years. My parents claimed they'd been quite happy with three boys before I came along as a "surprise." From day one, I was a fragile child and demanded a great deal of attention. Everything displeased me or made me cry. Only my maternal grandmother, whom everyone said I resembled, could entertain me with her fanciful tales. It was true that I was indulged, some might say spoiled, but who could blame me? This was how I was raised.

Where I come from, a daughter like me, a delicate daughter after three strong boys, was extravagantly cherished, perhaps more so because of my sensitivities. Of course, I was pretty enough, but I was also very smart, especially in math. From an early age, I could tell you the square root of high multiples in a matter of seconds. The numbers would appear to me as if spelled out in a clear blue sky. Teachers told my parents I had a gift. When I was in fifth grade, I began tutorials with a mathematics professor at the University of Tehran. I could be in college by now, had I insisted. But my mother worried that I would be socially stigmatized. This was considered a terrible blight for a girl in Iranian society. No matter how intelligent, no matter how ambitious, she is largely assessed by her ability to attract a good husband.

In short, my parents sent me to summer boarding school in Switzerland so that I could socialize with girls my age. *Girls from good families*, my mother stressed. *Girls with a future*. She thought it would be beneficial for me to share a room, make friends, get out from behind my books. She signed me up for tennis, sailing, archery, and advanced horseback riding.

Let me be perfectly clear: I had never before shared a room

with anyone. It came as an unpleasant shock. There was no nanny to unpack my trunks. No housemaid to run my bath and make certain the temperature was a welcoming degree of warm. There were supposed to be dances with a boys' boarding school. *Boys from good families,* Maman stressed. *Boys with a future.* I did not have any particular interest in boys beyond my brothers. What could they possibly offer me?

My first day was inauspicious. My plane was delayed by six hours, the airline lost one of my bags (the one with my Theoretical Physics textbooks), and the scheduled limousine never bothered to show up (I had to take a taxi all the way to the Swiss boarding school). By the time I arrived, everyone was eating dinner and I hurried to find my seat at a back table, clearly the least desirable.

As I ate my way, leaf by leaf, to the artichoke's soggy heart, I listened to the conversation around me. It was the same insecure litany of privileged progeny everywhere: what their fathers did for a living (bankers and industrialists, for the most part), the locations of their second and third homes (ski chalets in Gstaad; apartments in London; country homes in Provence), where they went to school (elite private institutions, naturally), and which cars they had been promised when they came of age (Porsches, BMWs, one Maserati). Honestly, I could not have been more bored.

For the first ten minutes, nobody bothered to ask me a single question. It was not until the second course arrived that people took notice.

"Do you eat pork?" a lumpy girl from Düsseldorf asked me.

Sometimes it was the only shred of pseudo-knowledge that Europeans exhibited about Muslims, or the Middle East.

I could have explained to her that my mother was of mixed heritage and my father a Muslim (and a prince, it so happened), that we celebrated both Christmas and Islamic holy days, that we served alcohol at home and at parties, and that yes, on occasion, we even ate pork. I could have told the girl from Düsseldorf all this, but the chances were it would not have changed her misinformed ideas.

"Yes," I said simply, cutting off a piece of pork and putting it in my mouth.

Everyone at the table turned to stare at me as I chewed, swallowed, and cut off another piece. *She speaks! She eats! What further wonders will this exotic creature exhibit for our entertainment?* This is what their facial expressions seemed to say. It was dully tiresome. As my father once chided me, I would have made a dreadful ambassador.

"She's lying," the Düsseldorf girl insisted. "She's just doing it to show off."

Nobody had ever questioned my integrity before, and certainly never over something as insignificant as a morsel of pork. Where I came from, my family's word was law. To question us, to imply that we were lying, was to insult us deeply. And to insult us meant to court imprisonment, or worse. Trust me, if the German girl had known this, she would have kept her mouth shut.

Things did not improve when I went to my room. The two best beds were already taken, and my bed was wedged against the front wall, where every footstep and squeal in the hallway was audible to me. I did not know what to make of my roommates. There was a plump girl from New York whose parents were from Cuba. It was not until I spotted her shelf crammed with books that I grew interested. The books, disappointingly, were novels. Frankly, I did not see the point of immersing oneself in fictitious worlds. It felt childish to me, like escaping into someone else's fantasy. When I tried to tell the Cuban girl this, she grew argumentative.

"I've learned more from fiction, more about truth and love than I've ever learned from real life," she said, waving around a copy of Sylvia Plath's *The Bell Jar.* Then she offered me a hazelnut truffle from a box of chocolates she excavated from her suitcase. I took this as a conciliatory gesture and accepted the truffle.

Our other roommate did not reappear until later that night. She introduced herself as Ingrid Baum and she was tall enough to be a Lebanese cedar. She wore ripped jeans and combat boots and a psychedelic T-shirt imprinted with JIMI HENDRIX IS GOD. When I inquired who Jimi Hendrix was, she looked at me as if I had put a multigenerational curse on her family.

"Where did you say you're from?" Ingrid demanded.

"Tehran."

"Don't you get television over there?"

"Of course."

"Don't you listen to music?"

"Yes."

"THEN HOW THE HELL CAN YOU ASK ME WHO JIMI HENDRIX IS, FOR CHRIST'S SAKE?!" She turned to Vivien, who was flipping through one of my quantum mechanics books. "Have YOU heard of Jimi Hendrix?"

"Sure. But I wouldn't exactly say he's God."

"I can't believe this!" Ingrid was beside herself and

stomped around the room in an unseemly manner. One could only imagine what this must have sounded like to the unfortunate girls in the room below us. "Okay, you two. Listen up."

She turned on her tape deck as loud as it would go. The ear-splitting music filled the room—a fast, grinding guitar accompanied by a voice so low and growling that it was impossible to decipher the words. I immediately thought of my brother Cyrus, unstoppable in his fighter jet, streaking across the sky. Forget the couture party dresses. Forget my matchmaking society mother. Forget teaching math to fidgety schoolgirls (the only respectable path for a smart girl like me). I wanted desperately to fly alongside Cyrus, screaming across the empty blue skies.

INGRID BAUM

We couldn't wait to get out of Canada—away from our town, away from our smothering German mother, and, frankly, away from *my* bad reputation. Our town was like a fish bowl. When you weren't swimming around inside it, fins ablaze and blowing bubbles, you were on the outside looking in, watching everyone else and making snide remarks. So when my little sister, Kathe, and I finally got on the plane in Toronto, I whooped and hollered so loud, the stewardess came over and read me the riot act. I got lots of dirty looks from the other passengers too. Apparently, airplanes were a lot more like small towns than we knew.

The first thing I did after the plane hit top altitude was whip out my fake ID and order a double scotch. I looked a lot older than fifteen. When I was dressed up and wearing makeup, grown men hit on me all the time. My sister was thirteen but looked about ten. She'd deny it, of course, but there was no way she could've ordered a double scotch and gotten away with it. So I poured some of mine into her Coke when nobody was looking and we both settled in to watch the movie—a crappy Hollywood flick dripping with sentimentality. When Americans weren't shooting up the universe, they were crying their eyes out over some sappy sob story.

I was more into absurdity. One bizarre thing juxtaposed with another. Sometimes I put my visions to paper. This made my mother worry to no end. When my father got back from his endless drives around Canada's ten provinces (he owned a factory that made portable fans and delivered them himself), Mutti would show him my latest sketches. Then I'd hear them whispering urgently behind their bedroom door. It was after my mother found a whole portfolio of my "disturbing" drawings that she and Vati decided to send me and my sister to Switzerland.

We'd never been away from home except for the time Mutti took us to visit her great-aunt Jutta deep in the Black Forest. Going there was like walking into a Grimm's fairy tale. Seriously scary. Our father had vowed long ago never to set foot in Germany again, so he didn't come with us. After World War II he got as far away as humanly possible from so-called civilization. That meant immigrating to Canada and finding the furthest semihabitable outpost in the northernmost reaches of Ontario province. We grew up in a massive log house that my father built with his own hands. It looked out over a pristine lake and was surrounded by an evergreen forest. Our closest neighbors were five miles away.

By the time we arrived in Geneva, I was fairly drunk. Luckily, Kathe was on the ball. She'd fallen asleep after that first spiked Coke, snoring loud enough for everyone in our immediate vicinity to complain. I had to shove her around until her head rested on my shoulder and the bulk of her snoring reverberated into my neck. That was my sister's saving grace: passing out before she could do herself, or anyone else, much harm. It was like having a safety valve embedded in her brain that switched off at a certain level of danger. Given that she hung out with me, this was probably a good thing.

Kathe got us through arrivals and customs (those Swiss guards really combed through our stuff) and out to meet the bus. I was tired but not tired enough to miss the good-looking boys gathering at the booth opposite ours. According to our glossy Pierpont brochures, we were supposed to have two dances with our so-called brother school, Le Rosey, a couple of miles away. Well, here they were less than twenty feet away and I wasn't about to squander the opportunity. I scanned the crowd and immediately settled on a tall, muscular boy with dirty blond hair and eyes as green as pond scum.

I went right up to him and asked him for a cigarette. He didn't have any so I offered him an unfiltered one of mine. "I think it's ridiculous to make up excuses to fraternize with members of the opposite sex, don't you?" I lit my cigarette and pulled a piece of tobacco off my front tooth. Then I held out my free hand until he shook it. "My name's Ingrid. I'm Canadian, of German descent, and bent on juvenile delinquency. And you?"

"Fyodor," he said, rolling his chiseled shoulders. "English, no speak little."

My best guess was that he was some kind of Russian wrestler son-of-a-diplomat kind of guy. I started feigning a few wrestling moves, the cigarette tight between my lips and swooning ash, which he found more perplexing than amusing. I was half hoping that Fyodor would be inspired to pin me down right there in the Geneva airport lounge when I heard a sharp voice calling my name.

"Mademoiselle Baum, come here this instant! We're ready to depart!" The voice belonged to our trusty chaperone, Mademoiselle Pinot, a prune of a woman I suspected I'd have a few run-ins with before the summer was through.

Before I could get into a lusty headlock with my hunky, minimally verbal Russian, Mademoiselle Pinot whisked me off to the company of Pierpont's other happy campers. Reluctantly I dragged my sister to the back of the shuttle bus, which I considered the best vantage point for checking out our fellow travelers. There were thirteen of us onboard, not including Mademoiselle Pinot and the twitchy driver with his patent-brimmed hat. I looked around and tried to guess who might become my friend that summer. It wasn't promising. Everyone looked too neat, too well behaved, too *boring*.

Before I'd left Canada, my father told me that this trip to Europe might turn my life around, that I could become anyone I wanted to be. It'd certainly worked for him, but in the opposite direction. He'd left Europe after World War II and went from being a Nazi soldier to a wildly successful manufacturer of portable fans. So what was he expecting from me? That I'd undergo a metamorphosis from "adventurous artist" (their kindest description of me) to some French-speaking dilettante? Fat chance. Sometimes I felt forced to go to extremes just to ensure some negotiating room. *Okay, so you're telling me I can't go to art school in Toronto? Would you prefer I become a heroin addict instead?*

The Swiss boarding school was super fancy. Chandeliers everywhere and a common room with leather sofas and backgammon boards inlaid with mother-of-pearl. I counted eight tennis courts, an Olympic-size swimming pool, and dedicated studios for everything from pottery to cooking. Apparently water ballet was mildly popular. I signed up just to see who the real idiots were on campus. I imagined going home and showing off my underwater pirouettes at the lake, Vaseline glistening on my teeth. Oh yeah, I'd be a huge hit.

In the dormitory, we were assigned our rooms. The younger girls, thirteen and under, were put on the first floor with resident counselors. Kathe really liked her roommates—a Ugandan girl whose father was a deposed foreign minister; and a flighty girl from Barcelona who had a suitcase filled with chewing gum. The fourteen- and fifteen-year-olds lived on the second floor, with a TV lounge to themselves. Sixteen- and seventeen-year-olds lived on the third floor with fancier accommodations—private rooms and baths, and daily maid service. And the few rooms on the fourth floor were strictly reserved for eighteen-and-ups. (Who the hell would be going to summer camp at eighteen? Beyond pathetic, if you ask me.)

I got to my room before anyone else, so I staked out the bed by the window. It would come in handy if I needed to sneak out at night to meet my Russian wrestler. Ha! The window overlooked too-perfect gardens and a big, burbling fountain featuring a trio of dopey-looking Greek goddesses holding water jugs. If I'd had a BB gun, I would've aimed for their marble noses on the spot.

After dinner, I sneaked off campus for a couple of hours to check things out. Nobody missed me in the confusion of the first day. Actually, I was trying to figure out where the boys' school was in relation to ours. Why the big separation? Just because we were old enough to get pregnant didn't mean we should be kept apart from the XY chromosomes. Boys made up half the human race, so what was the big fucking deal? To act like they were kryptonite only made things worse. Everyone back home was sure that I'd had sex already. I hadn't, but I was determined to that summer. In my experience, grown-ups always kept the best stuff for themselves.

DAY FOUR

VIVIEN

Dear Mom,

Sorry I haven't written to you sooner but it's been nonstop
since I arrived. French is okay, but my favorite class—
surprise!—is cooking. Our teacher, Monsieur d'Aubigné,
was a chef at a four-star restaurant in Paris before the place
burned to the ground. (He swears it wasn't his fault, no
matter what the newspapers said.) Ceramics is fun, too, kind
of like cooking except you don't get to eat what you make—
ha, ha! Horseback riding and waterskiing are HARD.

I'm still getting used to my roommates. It's like having two
stepsisters you've never met before suddenly come into your
life and take over the bathroom. We're supposed to have our

*first soiree this weekend and I'm hoping the boys here can
actually dance. That's the one thing I miss about Miami.
Those Cuban boys could really MOVE. Have you heard
from Tía Cuca and Abuela Gloria? Please send them
besitos for me—and take some for you, too.*

Love,

Vivien

*P.S. Care packages with anything chocolate in them are
welcome!*

It was searingly hot in the kitchen. Chef d'Aubigné didn't
believe in starting us with easy dishes. He said if we couldn't
learn how to make a cheese soufflé in one afternoon then
we might as well hang up our toques and "leave it to the
masters." That was one of his regular, disdainfully uttered
phrases, along with "flambés are for showmen, not chefs,"
and "hamburgers, *mes petites gourmandes,* are not food."
He added *mes petites gourmandes* to nearly every sentence,
underscoring the seriousness of cooking, which, according
to him, "is a sacred calling, like the priesthood, not a mere
profession." After just two meetings, Chef d'Aubigné had
driven half the class to tears and/or to desperately switching
into the one available class left in that time slot: Enameled
Brooch-Making.

Every aspect of *performing* the cheese soufflé was of
utmost interest to Chef d'Aubigné: the quality of the butter;

the balance of the béchamel sauce; the consistency of the grated Gruyère cheese; the freshness of the eggs ("if necessary, go inspect the chickens yourselves, *mes petites gourmandes*"); how to separate same eggs; how to whip the egg whites—but not overly—into firm, perfect peaks; how to grate nutmeg; how to properly butter a soufflé dish or any other baking pan; the woeful unreliability of most kitchen thermometers; the varieties and relative merits of peppercorns. And this was all *before* we put the soufflés in the ovens.

Chef d'Aubigné exhorted us to be ever-vigilant of our soufflés through the oven window, making sure their "blossomings" were progressing evenly. All the while he regaled us with stories about hunting for autumn truffles with his beloved pig, Coco ("ze greatest snout in ze field"), or helping his farmer parents stuff their prized geese, whose livers would end up as silky foie gras.

Everyone thought Chef d'Aubigné was out of his mind but I loved his uncompromising standards. I wanted to grow up to *be* him, minus the moustache and swiveling pot belly, of course. I, too, felt the sacred calling. I, too, longed to reach the pinnacle of culinary achievement, to serve my creations with sprigs of fresh rosemary, or patterned dustings of confectioners' sugar.

"Now let us synchronize our watches, *mes petites gourmandes*. How many minutes until your masterpieces are ready?"

We all checked the prominently ticking clock on the kitchen wall.

"*Mais, non!*" he screamed, clutching his heart, as if someone had stabbed him with the filleting knife. "Never rely on mechanics to tell you when your dish is done. Use your eyes and your nose, your ears and ze fingertips. Is that clear?"

"It's not like the soufflés can talk," mumbled a sullen Danish girl named Gerta. She'd had about all she could take.

Everyone gasped, waiting for Chef d'Aubigné's reaction. His lids dropped to half-mast and he was as motionless as a lizard. The silence seemed to last forever. Then, to our surprise, he put his arm around Gerta and steered her toward the gargantuan oven.

"Uh-oh, here comes the big Hansel and Gretel moment," stage-whispered Tiffany, an overly tanned girl from L.A. "The Danish kid's going in the oven."

Instead, the chef, with a sweep of his arm, indicated the budding soufflés.

"*Au contraire*, my little monkey. The soufflés are talking to us all the time. 'Rise, we are rising,' they say. Or 'Look how beautifully golden we've become. We are counting on you mere mortals not to deflate us.'"

Everyone began to titter.

Chef d'Aubigné turned to face the class. "Who among you dares to speak intimately with these goddesses?"

Tentatively I raised my hand.

"Mademoiselle Wahl?"

"I'll talk to them, Monsieur."

"Very well."

I went up and took Gerta's place by the oven, peered in at the luscious perfection of our soufflés.

"Oh, you're such buttery little soufflés," I ventured uncertainly as the class started giggling again.

"Go on," Chef d'Aubigné encouraged me.

"I see you're getting, uh, quite puffy and . . ." This was actually much more embarrassing than I'd imagined.

"Sexy!" Tiffany shouted out, and everyone laughed.

I ignored her and continued sweet-talking the soufflés. "Are you ready to come out yet?" I coaxed, feeling strangely elated. Was I imagining their collective sigh of *"Oui"*? With conviction, I turned to Chef d'Aubigné and triumphantly announced: "The soufflés say they're done."

SHIRIN

The quality of the horses at the Pierpont Boarding School for Girls left much to be desired. Scruffy and dyspeptic. Ill-groomed and excessively flatulent. Unsuitable for serious riders in every respect. I was accustomed to my sleek Arabian stallions. Why should I be forced to lower my standards for the dubious prospect of making a transient friend or two?

My hapless mother fretted endlessly about my antisocial nature. All through primary school, she refused to accept that I was happiest playing alone or with my brother Cyrus. I rarely went to birthday parties and did not invite friends over after school. I was definitely not the daughter my mother had hoped to raise. In Iran, certainly in my family, nobody enjoyed being alone. It was considered aberrational, even hostile, like an unwelcome physical flaw.

That was not to say that decent equestrians did not exist in the advanced horseback riding class at Pierpont. There was one quite fine rider, a British girl who had probably started riding before she walked, and another who excelled at the high jumps. But everything about horseback riding in Switzerland was regulated, inhibited, dreary. Who among them had stampeded across a desert, utterly free?

As I trotted around the ring, putting my anemic horse through its paces and desultory jumps, I thought of my brothers scattered around the globe and wondered when we would be reunited again. It seemed odd that our parents exhorted us to go out in the world, as it kept us separated for months on end. The youngest (and my favorite) brother, Cyrus, was nearly a decade older than me but we were very close. He alone knew what I was capable of. He alone appreciated my intelligence. With him, I could laugh most freely, be the silliest version of myself.

After six days at the Swiss boarding school, things were hardly ideal. Almost nobody deigned to talk to me and my Canadian roommate had the audacity to call me "fucking haughty" when I asked her to turn down her barbaric music one night. She could not have gotten away with saying this to me back home. Depending on who her family was, she might have landed in one of the shah's dungeons for considerably less. There were two other Iranian girls here, inseparable childhood friends two years younger than me. We were of no interest to each other whatsoever.

In most ways, the rules for everything were not so different in Switzerland than in Iran. People cared furiously about family position, money, and so forth. But the prejudices against my country usurped all logic and civility. To many, I was nothing but a wealthy petro-savage. If I had shown up with a bone through my nose, they probably would not have been surprised.

At the horseback riding ring, I saw Vivien in the beginners group comically trying to post. Her posterior was sufficiently pronounced that it made no difference—to the naked eye, at least—whether or not she lifted herself out of the saddle. She waved at me energetically and I managed to return a wan smile. In the evenings, Vivien mostly buried herself in her books, as did I. We skipped after-dinner activities: the backgammon tournaments and talent shows, the tedious documentaries on Switzerland's long-standing policy of political neutrality.

Once, I sat through fifteen stultifying minutes of such a film before fleeing to the semireassuring war zone of our room. Ingrid was a nightmare—rude, aggressive, inconsiderate, and with the worst taste imaginable. *She* was the true barbarian here. Vivien was polite enough but she seemed immeasurably more interested in comestibles than serious ideas. Rumors were rampant that she had been heard talking to her soufflés in cooking class.

After horseback riding, Vivien and I found ourselves sitting next to each other on the bus back to campus. The acrid smell of both quadrupeds and bipeds permeated the air.

"You were amazing," Vivien gushed. "You're practically an Olympic rider."

"No, I am not," I said, trying not to feel too pleased. "But I have been riding a long time. I saw you, too."

"Please don't be nice."

"I was not planning on it," I said. To my surprise, Vivien did not take offense. Either she did not register my sarcasm, or chose to ignore it. In any case, she continued talking, as she always did.

"My horse, Gitaine the Third . . . why can't they come up with different names for them, anyway? It's so confusing. He didn't listen to a thing I said. If I pulled on his reins, he went faster. If I dug in my heels, he slowed down. It was nuts. I just wish they'd let us get out and ride in the woods or something. Going around in circles makes me nauseous."

"Back home, I almost never ride in a ring."

"Where do you go?"

"To the Alborz mountains, north of Tehran. In early spring, the meadows are most exceptional, dazzling with poppies and other wildflowers. Or sometimes I traverse the desert in wintertime. That is when you can really fly."

Vivien sat wide-eyed, enduring the bumpy bus ride, attempting to envision what I was telling her. But it was impossible to imagine unless you have experienced the beauty firsthand. In the spring I rode through endless carpets of intoxicating flowers. I especially loved the little flames of poppies, martyred in their fields. And there was nothing like the vivid striations of sunrise in the desert, hopeful as salvation. I wondered how many places were left on the planet where one could race across the land on a galloping horse for fifty unbroken miles. Cyrus told me once that only the skies promised infinity anymore. That was another reason why he loved being a pilot.

"Would you like to go riding together sometime?" I offered. "Outside of the ring?"

"Do you think they'd let us?" Vivien asked.

"Why not? It beats riding around in this heat and stink."

"What the hell is that stench, anyway?" Vivien laughed. "It's like someone died in here."

I looked around at the flawless complexions of our bus-mates, their damp hair and armpits, their grimy clothes and dirt-caked boots, all of which soon would be thoroughly washed and shined to glossy perfection.

DAY
TEN

INGRID

Okay, so it started out as a joke but then I was trapped big-time. There was nothing I could do except bail on the whole Swiss summer thing. And my parents would've flipped out if I'd done that. I begged the powers that be to let me switch out of water ballet into *anything* else, including macramé. But the answer was an unequivocal no. Skipping it didn't do me any good, either (believe me, I tried) because totalitarian house arrest ensued. Who knew that the Swiss could be even more anal-retentive than Canadians?

Misery was nose clips, a dopey ballet bun, and thigh-twisting moves as hideous as they sounded—I mean, come on, the Egg-beater? Misery was having Madame Delfin, the instructor, make us hold our breath underwater until our lungs burst. Misery was five other chirpy girls under five-foot-four who actually adored the sport. The worst of the lot was Midori Shibuya, who hailed from Tokyo and was a competitive machine in chlorine. Believe me when I say I swallowed enough pool water those first few days to single-handedly rehydrate the Gobi Desert.

Everything was wrong, all wrong. This wasn't the summer of freedom I'd imagined. My sister, damn her, was doing just fine. She was getting along with her roommates, practicing her French, and becoming multiple teachers' pet. Kathe turned out to be a naturally gifted tennis player, too. She jumped up four levels in no time and was competing against the best seniors. For the first time in her life, my sister was independent. I accused her of avoiding me but Kathe only shrugged and said,

"I've been busy."

I, on the other hand, didn't fit in anywhere. It was like I'd landed in a distant galaxy with the most unbendable rules in the universe. *Welcome to Planet Switzerland, where even your bodily emissions must conform to quality standards.* Shit. What the hell was I doing there? I was the worst in my French class, couldn't get the hang of any sports, and nobody wanted to do anything remotely fun or exciting. For that, I could've stayed in Ontario and screwed moose.

"Remember, ladies, you are not clumsy sea mammals," Madame Delfin warbled above the roller rink music she blasted at us by the pool. "*Interpret* the moves. *Impress* me with your artistry. Everyone, follow Midori. Especially you, Ingrid."

Instead I attempted to follow Mercedes (Spanish) and Siri (Finnish) into a reverse scoop, flooding my sinuses and what was left of my sodden brain.

"You're breaking the circle, Ingrid. I repeat: 'Follow

Midori.' Now segue gracefully into the flamingo position. The flamingo, Ingrid, not the crane!"

I felt like a goddamn pterodactyl, flailing around in the water on the verge of extinction. I looked around contemptuously to see who I could take down with me. The golden, turbo limbs of water ballet-poster girl, Midori, beckoned. I caught her eye and she made the fatal mistake of sneering at me. I ignored Madame Delfin and her high-sheen, waterproof makeup and submerged myself like a barracuda. In a spangled flash, I had Midori by an ankle and was dragging her toward the deep end of the pool. Down, down, down we went. I could tell by her bug-eyed look that she was terrified. I was no longer responsible for my actions.

There was a great commotion above us but it seemed remote to me, in slow motion. Without warning, I felt pincers on my shoulders like a couple of giant lobster claws. It was Madame Delfin, come to rescue her star pupil. I put up a valiant fight against evolutionary obliteration and managed to slug Madame Delfin in the eye. She bared her teeth. Her lips looked hugely red and magnified underwater. It was just as well I couldn't hear her.

Midori dolphin-kicked to safety and it was me and that water ballet teacher in a titanic battle for our lives. Madame Delfin played dirty and gave me a swift kick in the solar plexus with her manicured foot. Then, before I could react, she immobilized me between her steel-trap thighs and pulled me back up to the surface. The other girls were screaming like I'd murdered someone, and Midori was melodramatically gasping for air. I was wiped out, waterlogged. Only the shrill sound of Madame Delfin's whistle cut through the chaos.

Word got around fast about my attempted murder of Midori and Pierpont's illustrious water ballet teacher. It was a bad scene—calls to my parents, an ugly face-to-face with the headmistress, Madame Godenot (during which I found myself studying evidence of sun damage on her nose and cheeks), testimonies galore from every water-inclined nymph in the place, threats of expulsion, a spell of detention in the library. I was given official written warning of my impending suspension if I did not remediate my attitude *tout de suite* and become an exemplary member of the Pierpont community. Blah, blah, blah.

One good thing came of this, besides getting to take a swipe at Madame Delfin: Overnight, I became a celebrity—glamorous, elusive, dangerous. Suddenly everyone wanted to be my friend. Down the hall, the hardcore partiers came by with their high-grade dope and tabs of acids (I took a few hits from the former; declined the latter.) Even the popular girls were knocking on our door to hang out. One of them, a Swedish goddess named Ursula whose father was a famous film director, suggested we trade outfits for a day. She got to wear my ripped jeans and Rolling Stones T-shirt. I opted for her steel blue one-piece jumpsuit that made me look like a goddamn astronaut.

Everyone, I concluded, loved a renegade. Everyone, that is, except my two roommates, who already had reservations about my sanity—and, apparently, their safety.

"I will sleep with one eye open and I recommend you do the same," Shirin advised Vivien. "She may very well be capable of asphyxiating us while we sleep. Might I suggest we repose without pillows?"

"My father slept with a gun on his nightstand," Vivien

offered. "My whole family was on a hit list for a year."

"No shit. How come?" I asked. I'd never known anybody on a real hit list before. It made conventional Swiss boarding school brutality seem juvenile by comparison.

"Homicidal maniacs."

"She knows all about that then, does she not?" Shirin continued to refer to me in the third person.

"I know how to shoot a gun, too," Vivien addressed her remarks to the hostile no-fly zone between me and the Iranian princess. "My father taught me."

"That is very reassuring," Shirin said, getting into bed with one of her massive textbooks. "Let us hope you will not need to employ your self-defense skills this summer. I, for one, have only the weight of mathematics to save me." She hoisted her textbook in my direction then turned away with a huff.

"We had to check under our cars for bombs every morning," Vivien continued. "At one point, my dad hired a bodyguard to walk me to and from school. That's why we finally left Miami."

"Whoa." I'd definitely underestimated Vivien. I dug into my suitcase for my battered carton of cigarettes and pulled out a fresh pack. I tapped it against my open palm and offered her a cigarette. To my surprise, she accepted one and didn't cough nearly as much as the first time. She was tougher than I thought.

"Are those Marlboros?" It was Shirin, her back still turned to us.

"Yeah. You want one?" I took the high road and walked over to her bed to make my peace offering. She took the cigarette and silently accepted my light. Then the princess inhaled like her lungs were in her toes and blew out the smoke, replicating the rings of Saturn. I whistled in appreciation. Here was something we could finally agree on.

"How'd you learn to do that?" Vivien asked, her eyes watering.

"Three." Puff. "Older." Puff. "Brothers." Double puff.

We sat there smoking for about ten minutes, not saying much, but growing more comfortable in one another's presence. Our window was open. The moon was half full and floating like a yellow grin in the sky. Something subtle and sweet-smelling rose up from the garden, cutting through our smoke. I didn't know what my roommates were thinking but I had this quiet, happy feeling over nothing in particular. We were just three girls finding, temporarily, someplace to relax and be ourselves. Maybe, I thought, just maybe, we could become friends.

DAY
FOURTEEN

INGRID

I was riding high on my newfound celebrity. In the evenings
our dorm room was the place to be, much to the astonishment
of Vivien and the diminishing annoyance of the Iranian princess. One thing was undeniable: I'd become the ultimate arbi-
ter of cool at Pierpont—fashion, social relations, daringness,
musical taste. Even my sister and her tennis friends basked in
my reflected glory. Celebrity, though, had its price. I was down
to my last pack of cigarettes, the acolytes had guzzled all my
booze, and wanna-be-me's were affecting my toughness with
ripped T-shirts, jeans, and combat boots they'd rustled up who
knows where. It was downright perturbing to see myself thus
mirrored.

Heightening the excitement was the upcoming garden party,
the first of the summer. The drama quotient was off the charts

and I probably would've skipped the whole damn thing if it weren't for the lingering picture of that monosyllabic Russian wrestler with the eye-catching pectorals. Or so I daydreamed. I'd never been popular before—only feared and avoided—so it was with no small sense of burden that I plodded toward Saturday night's dance. What I realized fairly quickly was that boldness trumped ordinariness every time. People didn't admire me for run-of-the-mill rebelliousness. They wanted the jaw-dropping, corporeal action that could lead to death.

Of course, everyone also wanted to know what I was going to wear to the dance, who I would hang out with, how far to go with the boys, and whether I would let fly another attack on the water-ballet wunderkind or Madame Delfin, the night's designated chaperone-in-chief.

An hour before the party, our room was wall-to-wall with Pierpont's finest. Everyone was struggling to get dressed, putting on makeup and high heels, and commenting—with varying degrees of cattiness—on one another's outfits. The air was choked with deodorant, hairspray, and tear-inducing clouds of expensive perfume. There was furious swapping and bargaining going on: these gold hoop earrings for that suede belt; your thigh-high boots for my peek-a-boo mesh top; the push-up bra for your electric green eye shadow.

I had this image of us fusing into one big blob of fragrant, oversexed adolescence and devouring the boys whole, like in some horror movie. Ursula, my new lieutenant, was controlling access to the bathroom, the most crucial post of the preparty preparations. I think she definitely inherited her director father's propensity for bossiness. Vivien was getting into the spirit of things but Shirin just sulked on her bed, peeking out from behind a copy of *Aerospace Today* when she thought no one was looking.

I guess it was only a matter of time before utter pandemonium broke out. A Moroccan girl and her Syrian friend got into a fight with two Italian sisters over blue eyeliner. As I was trying to physically separate them, it turned into a bigger, nastier brawl involving seventeen hormonally deranged Pierponters. The partial tally of injuries: a swollen eye, myriad face scratches, a fistful of pulled hair, one puncture wound by tweezer, four broken nails, and a twisted ankle. I had to kick everybody out and was left, panting, with only my trusty roommates.

"I can see diplomacy is not your strong point," the Iranian princess quipped. I could always count on her for a dose of sarcasm. She wasn't bothering to dress for the dance. In fact, she wasn't planning to go at all.

"It wasn't her fault." Vivien came to my defense. She seemed energized by the fighting. Maybe it reminded her, nostalgically, of her fractious youth in Miami.

"Border disputes. Nuclear proliferation. The battle for outer space." Shirin sighed, settling into bed with another one of her doorstop textbooks. "Arguably, *those* are worth going to war over. But mascara?"

"It was eyeliner." I shrugged. "Never underestimate the inflammatory power of cosmetics."

"Why don't you come with us to the party, Shirin?" Vivien tried another tack. "We'll miss you if you don't."

"Yeah, who else can we count on to slice-and-dice the little people?" I chimed in, digging through my drawers and my still-half-unpacked suitcase for something I could wear. Finally, I found the sixties flower-power minidress I'd salvaged from a thrift store in Toronto. Damn, I should've bought those white vinyl go-go boots when I had the chance. That would've freaked everybody out. Another thing I learned about celebrity: you had to keep everyone guessing.

The fracas-inciting eyeliner had rolled behind the toilet and I used it now, smearing it in a thick line above my eyelashes and out into swirled peaks on my temples. "What do you think?" I asked my roommates; though an icon wasn't supposed to elicit anyone's opinion, simply pronounce her own.

"Cool!" Vivien said.

"Are you planning on conducting an interplanetary space mission?" Shirin asked, barely looking over the top of her book.

"Huh?" Vivien was confused.

"I think she means that I look like I'm heading off to Mars."

"Touché for the Canadian."

"Can I borrow some?"

"Sure, Viv." I tossed her the eyeliner. The top wasn't screwed on tight and a kidney-shaped cluster of navy droplets spattered her comforter.

Shirin conspicuously turned a waxy page but I could tell she was enjoying this.

"Christ, I'm sorry," I said, and meant it. Vivien was turning out to be my one loyal friend in this craziness.

While we were washing out the eyeliner with wet towels, a whinnying cry started in the gardens, reverberated down the hallways of the Pierpont Boarding School for Girls, and permeated the pink, pubescent hearts of every girl on campus: "They're here!" The bus from Le Rosey had arrived and was, at that very moment, unloading its rich hormonal lode of hot-blooded international males.

Even the Iranian princess couldn't help abandoning the heady diversions of high-powered mathematics to peer out our room's only window and assess the incoming goods. They were beautiful, these boys, smooth-skinned and shiny-haired, freshly showered for our olfactory pleasure. Most of them wore blue blazers and gray slacks and the skinny, tasteful ties given to them by their grandmothers. A couple of the boys wore leather jackets—not renegade black, but expensive, buttery brown—and one biceped wonder came dressed, intriguingly, as a Venetian gondolier. I looked past them, squinting toward the dark womb of the bus to see if I could spot my hunky Russian wrestler. Alas, he was nowhere to be found.

VIVIEN

The dance was called a garden party even though it was mostly indoors, artificially lit, and without so much as a daffodil in sight. Sometimes when a phrase in English doesn't make sense to me, I translate it into Spanish. *Fiesta de jardín.* For me, it's a way of pulling words and meanings apart into their constituent elements, giving them a new context and rhythm. Growing up speaking two languages has come in handy. Not just for whispering secrets, but for cultivating perspective, a certain distance between you and what you're observing. It's like sitting on a stone

CRISTINA GARCÍA

wall between two countries, two cultures, two gardens, but
not fully participating in either.

Ingrid sent me down to the dance early as her scout. She
wanted me to "check out the merchandise," as she put it, and
return with a complete report before she and her entourage
descended to the party. I was happy to oblige. Before my dad
became a pariah in Miami, parties were a way of life. Cubans
partied with a vengeance. They'd partied in Cuba and when
they arrived in Miami, they continued to party. Not a single
weekend went by that someone wasn't celebrating a birthday
or a christening, an anniversary or a wedding. No matter how
bad things got, cutting down on fun wasn't an option.

While the girls were upstairs, hysterical with last-minute
preparations, I headed to the ballroom to find about sixty
boys milling around and looking uncomfortable. A few of the
younger, less popular girls were already there but nobody
was paying much attention to them. The boys clumsily
served themselves punch, chatted with our chaperones, and
nervously cracked jokes. All eyes turned on me as I entered
but I could see their hopes dashing like a crashing row of
dominoes. I thought I looked pretty good in my yellow party
dress but I guess I wasn't the calendar pinup they were hoping for. My heart sank. Why did I bother?

I scanned the room, remembering my mission, and picked
up specifics to report back to Ingrid. To me, the boys were
hard to tell apart. Nearly all of them wore the same navy blue
blazers with golden crests on their pockets. Actually, they
were pretty gorgeous.

"Where are the other girls?" Madame Delfin demanded,
sotto voce. Then she curled her upper lip—I think it was an

attempt at a smile—at a spindly boy with braces. She was even scarier looking up close than Ingrid had described.

"Oh, they'll be right down," I said cheerfully.

"Would you kindly go upstairs and request their immediate presence in the ballroom?" Then she leaned in close. "Don't you know it's rude to keep guests waiting?" (Was I imagining her flounder breath?)

A chubby, dark-skinned boy with thick eyebrows gave me a hesitant smile. His hair was so glossy—naturally, or by brilliantine, I couldn't tell which—that he reminded me of the seals at the Miami seaquarium. If I'd had the forethought to bring a beach ball, I would've tossed it to him. Instead I grinned stupidly back. Madame Delfin followed my expression to his then glared at us both.

"Tout de suite!" she barked.

Before I could head upstairs to alert the troops, they paraded—*slinked* might be a better word—into the ballroom in undulating waves of perfumed, tittering glory. Ingrid led the way in a psychedelic minidress that made her legs look two miles long. Neon peace signs the size of dessert plates dangled from her ears and her hair was poufed out like a model's. Someone turned up the music about five thousand decibels. The boys lurched forward, half stunned by all the well-bred beauty on display, and the garden party began.

SHIRIN

I was not planning on going to the garden party. It was the last thing I wanted to do. Back home, my mother was an inveterate party thrower. She didn't need a pretext. Nearly every day after school I would find a group of her friends gathered in the living room drinking tea and eating sweets off her best French china. Another set of friends or relatives would invariably come for dinner. And at least three or four nights a week, my parents entertained late into the night. My presence was expected at these never-ending affairs. Maman wanted to show off how much I had grown, or my latest academic achievements, or my precision-drill English. I would be forced to endure the pinched cheeks and cloying compliments for an eternity.

It was solitude I craved most of all. No, that is not quite right. It was my brother Cyrus's company I craved most of all. I could spend hours talking to him about everything under the sun, or say nothing at all. We were that comfortable together. Solitude came a distant second.

Anyway, I had been enjoying a quiet evening in our dormitory room when I heard a soniclike boom at a quarter after eleven, followed by sustained shrieking. I felt compelled to investigate. I knew from experience that it was prudent to ascertain the nature of an explosion before continuing with one's business. In Tehran, bombs went off with alarming frequency despite the government's vigilance. There were many people unhappy with the direction the shah was taking the country.

I brushed my hair and put on the dove gray taffeta dress my mother had packed for fancy occasions. Then I headed down to the ballroom, not knowing what I would find. To be honest—my mother liked to say that only children and fools are honest—my curiosity had gotten the better of me.

The ballroom was dark and hazy and a grinding song I

had not heard before was playing deafeningly loud. One of the loudspeakers was smoking in the corner, most likely the source of the explosion. Many of the boys and girls were fused together at the edges of the dance floor, kissing and groping each other madly. No chaperones were in sight and the paper decorations hung limply from the walls. Surely this was not what my mother had in mind when she rhapsodized about improving my "social opportunities."

I looked around, trying to find someone I recognized. The darkness, the unfamiliar bodies, and the slack, bleary faces made everyone look like they were ten feet underwater. It was unthinkable to me that people who had not known each other a few hours ago were so thoroughly exploring each other's topographies. I walked around tentatively, discomfited and fascinated. This was a world I had not encountered before. Ingrid's sister was awkwardly kissing a boy with a Brazilian soccer jersey under his blazer. Even the fat girl from Düsseldorf had found a mate, a snub-nosed boy who looked like her fraternal twin.

As I was about to exit, a blond athletic fellow grabbed my arm and pulled me to the dance floor. Immediately he pressed the full length of his body against mine and I could feel the muscles of his thighs and chest, the strength of his arms, a metallic pressure cutting against my hip bone. It occurred to me that this could be his penis, and it frightened me.

When I tried to disentangle myself, this boy, who had not so much as bothered to introduce himself, pushed me against the back wall, where numerous other couples were entangled. His face plunged toward mine so fast that I could not discern his face. If he were standing at a respectful distance from me today, I am quite certain that I would not recognize him.

His tongue roughly pried apart my lips and filled my mouth. I was stunned, immobilized. His lump of humid flesh swiped my own inert tongue. I tried moving my arms but he had them pinned to my sides. My legs felt heavy, as if they had been dipped in cement. His right hand climbed under my dress and slipped in my underwear. Before I knew what was happening, he jammed a finger inside me. It was awful, painful, but I was too shocked to cry. When the tip of his tongue grazed the back of my throat, I gagged. This caught him off guard and I broke away, stumbling toward the French doors to the gardens.

A cloud enshrouded the moon and a few faint stars were visible. The aroma of the flowers, a mixture of roses and jasmine, made me long terribly, crushingly, for home. I wiped my mouth with the back of my hand and spat into an elephant topiary. I wanted to brush my teeth twenty times, rinse away his foul taste. Shower for days to wash off his vile hands, the disgust I felt.

The cries started deep in my chest and waved upward, catching me unawares. I crumpled to the grass, staining my dove gray dress, feeling utterly disgraced. How could I face my parents after this? I was furious with them for sending me here, for not protecting me from this. I was desperate to go home, to see Cyrus again. I did not know how much time had passed before I heard the grunting a few meters away, behind a swan-shaped bush. It was the back of a tall boy, naked from the waist down, his slacks gathered around his ankles. He was thrusting forward and back like a manic piston.

There was someone else with him, a girl, on her knees,

her head moving contrapuntally with his muscular buttocks. I was hypnotized by the scene, unable to move, afraid to make sound. Then the boy arched his back and slumped over the girl's hair, groaning. A hot, rancid smell filled the air like a bitter cloud. The girl sat back, her face wet and glistening. In the moonlight, I recognized her. It was Ingrid.

DAY
NINETEEN

VIVIEN

My roommates were at war. There was no other word for it. It wasn't like the first week of hostilities, with its relatively good-natured sniping. The big freeze set in after the party with Le Rosey boys and nothing could make it right. Shirin told me that she'd seen Ingrid in the garden fellating some German guy. Ingrid didn't think it was such a big deal but Shirin refused to talk to her about it. Silence was her revenge and it was driving Ingrid crazy.

Apparently, Shirin wasn't the only one who'd seen Ingrid in *flagrante delicto*. Word spread quickly that she'd given a blow job to a complete stranger at the garden party. Soon Ingrid became a pariah to many of the girls who, a few short hours earlier, had championed her as their heroine.

Strangely enough, neither Ingrid nor Shirin put in for a

room transfer. There'd been a couple of notorious cases already, like the Norwegian girl who was violently allergic to Park Avenue Hope's spray deodorant and was rushed to the hospital in anaphylactic shock. Or the Spanish girl, Mercedes, who couldn't stand the stink of the dried squid her Korean roommate kept stored under her bed. But the war between Ingrid and Shirin was another order of combat altogether.

I think it might've been easier all-around if they'd actually bothered to speak to each other. At times deadening, at times tension-fraught, the silence was horrible. One night, Ingrid pulled a chair over to the foot of Shirin's bed and stared at her as she read. If she'd been wielding a knife and making threats on her life, she couldn't have been more provocative. For her part, Shirin no longer acknowledged Ingrid's presence. I'd never seen anyone act so coldly. In my family, when someone was upset, two minutes didn't go by without a major eruption. A lot of damaging things got said in the heat of the moment but the apologies flowed just as quickly.

After five days of warfare, I couldn't stand it anymore. I wanted to do something to break the stalemate. I used to perform magic tricks as a kid, especially after my father made his ill-advised trip to Cuba and ruined our life in Miami. I had this fantasy that if I could conjure a parrot, or hypnotize the gym teacher into acting like a donkey, then everyone would want to be my friend. I didn't have any props with me in Switzerland, but I hoped a trick or two might coax Ingrid and Shirin into being quasi-civil again.

"Who wants to be hypnotized?" I offered one night after the lights were out. The bitterness between them suffused the room like a noxious gas. It didn't help that Ingrid was smoking in bed, endangering our lives. The orange tip of her cigarette glowed in the dark like a tiny planet.

"What the fuck?" she said, exhaling loudly. But, inside her impatience, I detected a note of curiosity.

"No, I mean it." I forged ahead. "I've hypnotized everyone in my family, including my cat."

My approach was simple. I followed the script of a famous nineteenth-century hypnotist—*Think about everything and everyone that is precious to you . . .*—all the while swinging a cross or something religiously significant in front of the person's eyes. Once I hypnotized my grandmother and she confessed to a love affair she'd had with a lawyer from Seville in 1932. That was shortly *after* she'd married my grandfather. When she came to, Abuela Gloria denied everything.

"Did your cat refute everything, too?" Shirin asked icily.

"Yeah, I could see it denying eating your hyperactive canary or something," Ingrid chimed in.

The three of us started giggling but just as quickly stopped. For a moment, we'd forgotten that we weren't supposed to be having fun. No one said anything for a whole minute.

"Does anybody have a flashlight?" I asked.

Ingrid had brought her toolbox along to Switzerland. It wasn't like she was going around fixing the plumbing or anything, but she told me that she felt incomplete without it, kind of like how I felt when I wasn't wearing earrings. Mostly, she broke into the Pierpont kitchen, which she periodically raided for ice cream. Another time she sawed her way into the locked pool house and stole a pair of flippers (for a quick aquatic getaway, she said).

Ingrid's lit cigarette moved across the room and I heard a thud, then some clanging as she dug through her tools. The cigarette butt flew out the window and a beam of radiant light took its place. She could've lit up a football field with her industrial-strength flashlight.

"So, how do we start?" Ingrid shone the light under her chin, giving her an eerily deranged appearance.

"Do you have a crucifix?" I asked.

"What, do you think I kill vampires in my spare time?" Ingrid snorted. "Next you're going to ask me for a braid of garlic, or a stake to put through my heart." She began to bounce the light around the room, like the laser shows I'd seen at the New York planetarium.

"I have something," Shirin said quietly.

I was grateful that she was interested at all. She reached under her silk pajama top. On the end of a delicate gold chain were several pendants: a filigreed cross, a silver Star of David, and a rectangle of gold-encased amber engraved in Arabic, which, Shirin said, was a prayer to the dead from the Koran. Carefully, she unhooked the chain from the back of her neck. It tinkled faintly as she handed it to me, glinting in the flashlight's bright beam.

"You're Jewish?" I wasn't sure why I was surprised. Jews were in the unlikeliest of places. If they sold jewelry in Cuba, like my dad, why couldn't they be in Iran?

"I'm a little bit of everything," Shirin said. "My family—"

"What are we waiting for?" Ingrid interrupted. "Are you going to hypnotize us, or not? We haven't got all night."

"I'll go first," Shirin said.

I could tell Ingrid was annoyed—no doubt, *she* wanted

47

to go first—but she kept her mouth shut for a change. She fixed the flashlight's beam on the pendants and lit another cigarette.

"Close your eyes," I instructed Shirin, lifting the pendants to eye-level.

"Oh, that's fucking rich," Ingrid sneered. "How the hell are you supposed to hypnotize her with her eyes closed?"

I ignored her. "Now think about everything and everyone that is precious to you," I continued my tried-and-true script. "Turn your feelings into liquid gold. Imagine bathing in that gold. Take your time. When you're ready, open your eyes."

Shirin's face relaxed, her taut jaw muscles visibly slackening. Her breathing grew slow and deep. My own breathing slowed down to match hers, and I had to catch myself from falling under my own spell. When Shirin finally opened her eyes, they looked a little glassy, filmed with tears. I wasn't sure whether or not to forge ahead, but her illuminated face encouraged me.

"Please fix your eyes on these pendants. Invite in the mystery and symbolism they contain." I moved my right hand slightly from side to side, swinging the chain like a pendulum before Shirin's gaze. "Open yourself to the unknown, to that which you only dimly perceive."

I could hear the chorus of crickets outside. They'd probably be mating in the damp grass all night long. I tilted my head toward the window to listen. I thought of the sweet Tunisian boy I'd danced with at the garden party. His name was Omar Belhassine and he'd asked if he could see me again. He was gentle and polite and at the end of the night, he'd nervously asked if he could hold my hand. It was warm and moist, and this made me like him all the more.

I turned to Shirin again. She seemed to be in a trance. Her eyes were wide open, transfixed by the pendants. Her lips were moving silently, as if in prayer. She had succumbed to hypnosis more easily than anyone I'd known. I wasn't sure what to do next. To make her act like some farm animal didn't seem appropriate or funny anymore. She looked so vulnerable, like a little girl. But I wasn't sure I wanted to hear some big confession, either.

Before I could suggest anything, tears began streaming down Shirin's cheeks.

"It's okay to return now," I said softly. "You can leave your place of sadness. You can leave it behind."

"Look how she's crying," Ingrid panicked. "Why is she crying?"

"I don't know but let me try to ease her out of it," I whispered.

Ingrid aimed her light beam on me, making me squint. Shirin's lips kept moving and words slipped out erratically, melodically, in Arabic or Farsi, I wasn't sure which. Then they started coming out faster and louder, like they were under some terrible pressure. Before we could stop her, she was shouting a scary torrent, her eyes riveted on the pendants.

"Jesus fucking Christ!" Ingrid barked and dropped the flashlight.

The room went black and all we heard was a heart-freezing, drawn-out, murderous scream. I ran to switch on the overhead light and saw Shirin, doubled over on her bed, crying uncontrollably, the sobs convulsing her body. Shuffling and shouts were coming toward us down the hallway.

I put my hand on Shirin's shoulder but she violently shrugged it off. "What? What happened?" I asked, desperate to make her stop.

"He's dead!" she cried wildly. "He's dead and I killed him!"

"What the hell?" Ingrid snapped.

"Be quiet," I ordered. "Give her time."

But Shirin wouldn't stop crying. She rambled on, possessed, mixing up languages and insisting that she'd been disgraced.

Ingrid and I looked at each other in confusion. We took Shirin's hands in ours and held them tight. Then without warning, Shirin grew utterly quiet, closed her eyes, and fell deeply asleep.

DAY
TWENTY-TWO

INGRID

It took a couple of days for things to resume some semblance of normalcy. Shirin, for her part, had no recollection of the hypnosis incident or anything that she'd blurted out. Vivien and I were afraid to press her under the circumstance and let the whole thing drop. I went on nightly ice-cream raids with my trusty tools and brought Shirin cartons of pistachio, her favorite flavor. Although things had somewhat calmed down with us, all hell was breaking loose outside our room.

Whoever thought that Switzerland was the epicenter of neutrality never spent time in a fancy girls' boarding school there. Vivien was accused of practicing witchcraft on defenseless victims, e.g. the Iranian princess. This made her the new celebrity at school, making official my precipitous deposition (I'd devolved from cool, aspiring assassin to full-fledged slut).

But Vivien's celebrity was the kind you definitely didn't want. Everyone avoided her, refused to sit at the same dinner table with her, tacked a filthy old broom on our dorm room door as a stupid joke. She considered leaving Pierpont altogether but Chef What's-His-Name and I convinced her to stay.

As if this weren't enough to deal with, my mother sent Kathe and me a telegram informing us that our father had crashed his car on a business trip to Alberta. Apparently, Vati fell asleep at the wheel on a stretch of isolated road and drove himself into a corn field. He got a bump on his head and was badly bruised. His tank of a car, a Swedish station wagon, sustained an equivalent amount of damage. He paid off the farmer and it was no big deal but my mother was sick with worry. She said Vati was behaving strangely, that he'd grown belligerent and forgetful and woke up terrified in the night, reliving his war years.

My mother put all this in the telegram that ended: SOMETIMES HE MISTAKES ME FOR THE ENEMY AND I HAVE TO PULL HIS HANDS FROM MY THROAT. LOVE, MUTTI. For Christ's sake, what kind of telegram is that to send to your daughters at summer camp? A part of me wanted to go back home and figure out what the hell was going on. A bigger part of me wanted to ignore her telegram altogether and hope the problem would simply vanish, like a bad dream.

Anyway, back to Pierpont. I figured that if my reputation was in the toilet, I might as well live up to it. At least the role was a familiar one. For the record, the lucky recipient of my blow job was not a *complete* stranger. He was a German boy named Joachim Silber and hailed from Munich, which also happened to be my father's hometown. Joachim and I flirted and danced for at least a half hour (much of it *auf Deutsch*) before he suggested we go outside. I figured we'd find a cozy place to make out when, to my surprise, he dropped his pants. I wasn't going to pretend I'd never seen a dick before, or even touched one. But when he nudged my head toward it, I felt unsure. This was something I *hadn't* done.

The worst wasn't the actual doing of it but what happened afterward. First, it so happened that Shirin was lurking in the bushes nearby and saw the whole thing. She didn't even have the courtesy to let me know she was there. What would it've cost her to cough a little? Secondly, Joachim didn't bother to say so much as *danke.* He simply zipped up his pants and walked away. I imagined him sidling up to his Le Rosey buddies inside and telling them what'd happened. *Arschloch.*

Everything started spiraling downward after that. I didn't feel I owed Shirin an explanation and, to her credit, she didn't ask for one. What she did do was start treating me like the scum of the earth. Swedish goddess Ursula also dropped me and everyone else followed suit. The day after the garden party, my fate was sealed. Only Vivien was still talking to me. My sister never mentioned it. Maybe Kathe hadn't heard the gossip (unlikely), or decided to ignore it. For that, at least, I was grateful.

It was Vivien's lame attempt at lessening the hostilities between Shirin and me that got her into hot water over this witchcraft business. It was radically weird, there's no denying that. My guess was that Vivien probably did have some paranormal psychic powers. But if she was a witch, she was a good witch, like the one in *The Wizard of Oz* who tried to save Dorothy from those creepy flying monkeys.

Partly as a reward for Vivien's loyalty and partly out of reckless abandon, I invited her to join me on a reconnaissance mission to Le Rosey. Vivien's family had suffered enough from blacklisting in Miami that she'd sworn never to inflict it on anyone—especially not over anything so insignificant. I didn't know how insignificant a blow job was, only that I was furious with Joachim and wanted to make him pay. I played revenge scenarios in my head. *What about a little reciprocity?* I imagined tormenting him, his arms tied behind his back. *What's the matter? Maybe you only like boys?* I was hoping for a last-minute bolt of inspiration.

Vivien was game to accompany me, for solidarity and sisterhood. Besides, she'd met some chubby North African boy she wanted to see again. No matter our proclivity for the opposite sex, Vivien decided that we were the only real feminists at Pierpont. Shirin was certainly smart enough to be a feminist but, in my book, she was way behind on the sexual liberation front.

We waited a good hour after lights-out to sneak off campus. Shirin was already raucously snoring in the corner. She'd taken to wearing earplugs and eyeshades to bed, as if the slightest noise might incite another psychotic break. I swear, that girl was a head case all by herself. Sometimes it seemed to me that Shirin wasn't just from another continent, but from another century; another galaxy, even.

Our dorm room was on the second floor so climbing out wasn't difficult. There were lights on in the teacher's quarters and the top floor of the dorm, where the oldest girls lived. Vivien and I were dressed in black, like burglars. "To merge with the night," I pronounced. I lent Vivien an extra pair of workmen's gloves so that she wouldn't scratch her hands maneuvering down the rose trellis. We figured it would take us about a half hour to trek the two miles to Le Rosey. If we were lucky, it might turn into an all-night adventure.

The smell of the garden was overpowering. I didn't know whether it was a scientific fact or not, but I suspected that the natural world did the bulk of its business after midnight. It never made sense to me that most human activity took place during the day. Everything was gentler at night, more forgiving. Every pockmark and blotch was dissolved. In the dark, you could become anyone you wanted to be. That night, I imagined I could hear the distant hum of the universe.

"Do you hear that?" I whispered to Vivien as we took cover behind a hedge.

"What?"

"The gods are smiling down on us."

I didn't need to see her face in the dark to know she was smiling back.

SHIRIN

It was the quiet that woke me. I was having that dream again, the one that started with my hypnosis. My brother was in the cockpit of his fighter jet flying high over Saudi Arabia. Between the cloudless skies and the endless stretch of desert, it was impossible to pinpoint his location. In the dream, I'm sitting in the copilot's seat, distracting him. First, I want to play backgammon. Then I pester him with questions—about theoretical physics, the stupidity of teachers, what it means to fall in love. Out of nowhere, that oaf from the garden party appears like a giant in the sky, his massive fingers smeared with blood. A missile comes hurdling at the fighter jet. My brother does not see it. I float out of danger like a ghost but Cyrus and his fighter jet are blown to pieces.

It was dark when I woke up, my heart jumping from the dream. Immediately I could tell that my roommates were not in their beds. I looked out the window just in time to see the unmistakable silhouettes of Ingrid and Vivien running toward Pierpont's front gates. I did not know what possessed me to follow them. It was as if someone else were directing my actions—an evil, unseen puppeteer.

I threw on some clothes and rushed downstairs, past the rooms of the younger girls, letting myself out the front door. Perhaps I was in a trance because my feet, hastily shod in riding boots, did not make a sound. Or rather, the sound they made was more of a swishing, like silk slippers gliding down a marble hallway. By the time I reached the front gates, Vivien and Ingrid were out of sight.

I turned right, imagining that I could catch their scent in the air like one of my father's hunting dogs. In reality, I did not have a clue about where I was going. The streets of Rolle were shut down for the night, peaceful in the way of Swiss villages. Nothing stirred, but I had the distinct sensation that I was being watched. I looked around at the quaint lamp-posts, at the sturdy shutters and stolid homes of these good Swiss citizens, and had a terrible urge to cause a disturbance.

Was I losing my mind? I had heard stories about how my maternal grandmother used to wander the streets of Tehran late at night, peering into strangers' windows. Often she had had to be brought back home by the police. Nobody ever talked about these incidents except in hushed, embarrassed tones. I assured myself that if I could question my own sanity, it was proof that I was, in fact, sane.

A rustling high up in a massive oak caught my attention. Perched on one of its uppermost branches—partly shrouded in leaves and utterly immobile—was the largest owl I had ever seen. Its eyes were luminously yellow, unblinking and fixed on me; its feathers gleamed a glossy, variegated brown. I had the discomfiting impression that it was assessing my potential as a late-night snack. I shuddered and kept moving, less certain of my mission. My footsteps echoed hollowly along the curb.

It was damp and cold. I had dashed out of the dormitory without a sweater. The skin on my bare arms puckered. I picked up my pace, no longer caring if anyone heard me. On the main street, a tourist shop displayed cuckoo clocks in its window, the pendulums furiously swinging out of synch. I was tempted to wait for the next hour's strike to see the flurry of shepherds and ubiquitous yodelers emerge from the minuscule doors. Down the block, the shoemaker's sign looked ominous with its oversize black boot. A sudden breeze made the rusty sign creak.

In the window of Le Pâtisserie Dubuffet, rows of marzipan were arranged on a glass shelf: perfect mini replicas of apples and mushrooms, fairies and bulbous-nosed gnomes. Suddenly, I felt an urgency to taste their sweetness. The shop door was locked but I tried to force it open. The silver lettering shimmered baroquely, taunting me. The army of large-nostriled gnomes sneered at me from their crisp rows.

The streets were swept clean, immaculately so, but behind

me a branch from that menacing oak unexpectedly crashed to the ground. I imagined that it was the owl offering me a gift, a possibility. Without hesitating, I grabbed the branch and dragged it back to the bakery. I squatted, lifting the heavy branch over my head. Then with all the force I could muster, I swung it around like a shot-put champion and hurled the oak branch through the window.

The shattering of the glass surprised me. I had not expected it to be so easy. Lights came on down the street and I heard muted voices from behind the shutters above the pastry shop. I had to act. Gingerly I reached in past the broken window and looted a handful of tidy marzipan gnomes. I did not notice my arm scraped to the elbow from the broken glass, ribboned with blood. I grabbed those gnomes and ran back to the Pierpont Boarding School for Girls, fleet-footed and invisible, biting off the first of a half-dozen heads, savoring the sugary glut of marzipan on my tongue.

DAY
TWENTY-FOUR

INGRID

It wasn't an unfamiliar place for me—specifically unfamiliar, yes, but not generally unfamiliar. I'd been in many principals' offices before, and had gotten kicked out of a fair share of them. My rap sheet wasn't exactly memo-length. An abbreviated tally: unruly behavior, disrupting classes, inciting rebellion (translation: cafeteria food fight), public drunkenness, destruction of school property (two dented garbage can lids and *tasteful* graffiti), corrupting minors (even though I was a minor myself), chronic truancy, pyromania (that fire was a total accident!), flagrant disregard of school rules (smoking, fashion adjustments to my uniform), et cetera, et cetera.

As we were about to sit down for our little chat, Madame Godenot was called away on an international phone call. This gave me ample opportunity to inspect her office. It was pretty much what you'd expect from a posh Swiss boarding school: expensive wood paneling, built-in bookcases, a somewhat tarnished antique globe. There was nothing personal in the room unless you counted the intricate model of an 1819 British clipper. It was rumored that the headmistress had been a sailing champion in her youth and was briefly married to a dissolute member of English aristocracy. She had no children.

When she returned, Madame Godenot filled the doorway with her considerable height. She settled behind her desk, waiting for her secretary to bring in a tray of mineral water. The headmistress's hands were remarkably small for a woman so tall, like chipmunk paws on a Great Dane. My hands were easily twice as big as hers. How had she managed to sail the world with those piddling fists?

"May I ask what you're thinking?" Madame Godenot began.

This caught me off guard. I couldn't exactly admit to marveling over her Lilliputian fingers so I said nothing.

"Do you know why you're here?" She tried a different tack.

Tack. That was a sailing term. A theme was emerging early in our discussion. I revisited the myriad reasons that might've landed me in her office again. Smoking indoors. Repeatedly breaking into the kitchen freezer. The now-notorious blow job in the garden. Sneaking off campus with Vivien for a late-night visit to the boys' boarding school. (That was a non-starter. We couldn't even get past Le Rosey's gates.)

"Are you aware that there was a break-in at Le Pâtisserie Dubuffet three nights ago?"

"Sure, I heard about it," I said noncommittally.

There'd been all sorts of crazy rumors about it but nothing substantiated. My personal favorite was that a deranged diabetic had smashed the window in a desperate suicide attempt. Apparently, a trail of headless marzipan gnomes—the only evidence in the case—was found leading to Pierpont's entrance. Really bizarre, even by my standards.

"Police reports indicate that witnesses spotted a young woman at the scene of the crime. I'm afraid her description closely matches yours. I want to warn—"

"What the hell?!"

"—you that I've contacted your parents. Again. I've requested that they retrieve you at the earliest possible moment." Madame Godenot pronounced *moment* in French, for extra emphasis.

"That's completely unfair! Who are those fucking witnesses? Don't I get to defend myself?" I'd been accused of many things in my life, but nothing as preposterous as this.

"I've spoken to the police commissioner," Madame Godenot proceeded as if I hadn't gone apeshit on her. She tapped a fingertip against the cream-colored folder on her desk. "We've come to an, eh, understanding of the situation. For the good of the school. For Pierpont's reputation."

"Yeah, well, what about *my* goddamn reputation?" I shrieked and my voice broke. Damn it, I didn't need to be embarrassed on top of being wrongly accused.

"That doesn't appear to be something you guard closely."

"What's that supposed to mean?" I was standing up by then, leaning over her desk. The bubbles from the mineral water floated up and tickled my nose. It was all I could do not to swipe everything off her desk. Or tear apart that British clipper of hers sail by precious sail. "Are you telling me that people get hanged around here by insinuation alone? Is that the Swiss justice system?"

Madame Godenot remained unruffled. I'd never seen such cool. Even in my fury, a part of me was impressed.

"The Swiss are not lenient with miscreants."

I glared at the headmistress but got stuck on the word *miscreant.* It lodged in my throat distastefully, like the acrid saliva that precedes vomiting.

"Where were you Thursday night? We already know you weren't in your room."

"I took a walk. I couldn't sleep."

"Off campus? Against school rules?"

"Sure, but that isn't a federal crime. And it doesn't make me guilty of a wacko pastry heist, either!"

Madame Godenot paused and looked at me directly, trying to gauge my trustworthiness. Perhaps she'd been underestimated when she was young and had wanted to sail around the Cape of Good Hope. This wasn't a case of underestimation, though; this was a case of exceedingly gross overestimation.

"Were you alone?"

"Yes," I said without thinking. There was no way I'd implicate Vivien. It was my mess and I didn't want to drag her into it. After all, it'd been my idea to try to storm Le Rosey and humiliate that München bastard Joachim. If anyone should be hauled into the headmistress's office, it should be Shirin. I'd noticed that her arm was suspiciously scraped up to her elbow. When I'd asked her about it, she pulled away from me without saying a word.

"You may not understand this now, but I'm doing you a favor, Mademoiselle Baum," the headmistress continued, her voice crisp as starched linen. "No charges will be brought against you. However, you will be kept on a minimal program for the next few days. Classes and meals only. No extracurricular activities. No overnight sailing trip on Lake Geneva. Your father has agreed to pick you up at his earliest convenience. This unpleasantness will soon be over."

"What about my sister?" I slumped down in my chair. Every muscle in my body ached, like I'd run a marathon, or swum the English Channel.

"Kathe is permitted to stay, of course. I'm not certain what your parents will decide."

"Shit," I said. "Fucking shit."

DAY
TWENTY-SEVEN

VIVIEN

It was sadly quiet for me without Ingrid around, as if every bit of life had gone out of our room, our floor, the entire school. I dragged myself from my French classes to my afternoon activities with no real sense of purpose. Worse still, there was no hope that anything remotely exciting would happen during our last week at Pierpont. Even the girls who'd hated Ingrid and gossiped behind her back seemed morose and lost without her, although none of them would've admitted it. Worst of all, my cooking class with Monsieur d'Aubigné had lost its allure.

Ingrid refused to say why she'd been kicked out. In fact, she refused to talk to anyone her last two days here. In the evenings she sat by herself on our windowsill, puffing on unfiltered cigarettes, blowing smoke rings out toward the stars.

Everyone speculated wildly about her expulsion. Was it the

blow job she'd given the German guy at the garden party? Had Midori's parents decided to sue the school over the near-drowning of their precious guppy? Was it Madame Delfin's complaints about her worsening asthma due to Ingrid's underwater attack? The smoking? The miniature bottles of airline booze?

Finally, word spread that Ingrid had been framed for the weird bakery break-in. I knew it wasn't true, because that night Ingrid and I had sneaked over to Le Rosey. Besides, she had absolutely no motive. Except for the occasional gallon of ice cream, Ingrid didn't eat sweets. Plus everyone knew about her toolbox. She could've broken into anywhere she pleased. There was no way she would've done something as sloppy as smashing a shop window with a tree branch. She was better than that.

I felt guilty that I hadn't gotten called into the headmistress's office alongside Ingrid. Whatever they accused her of, she certainly could've pulled me into it. But she didn't. She didn't rat anyone out. For that alone, she earned the respect of every girl at Pierpont. I promised Ingrid that I'd write to her, that I wanted her to visit me in New York. But she looked at me with a blank expression, and said nothing. I baked her a batch of madeleines for her journey back to Canada. She barely mumbled a thank-you.

When Ingrid's father showed up in a chauffeured limousine, everyone stopped what they were doing and gathered in the courtyard and on the dormitory balconies to watch. It was very unceremonious. No harsh words were exchanged. There was no drama, no crying or threats of vengeance, like would've happened in my family. We're talking exemplary stoicism. The only sign of life was when Kathe discreetly waved to her teary-eyed roommates.

Mr. Baum was a florid, portly man and wore a striped summer suit and shiny, coffee-colored shoes. He was as tall as Ingrid and you could tell that he'd been handsome decades ago, even with that bandage covering part of his forehead. He barely focused on his daughters and ignored the gawkers. Mr. Baum simply collected Ingrid and Kathe, instructed the chauffeur to put their luggage in the trunk, and without another word sped off down the long, oak-lined driveway of the Pierpont Boarding School for Girls.

That day, Ingrid looked smaller to me than she'd ever had; nothing like the giantess who'd first greeted me in our room with a pack of cigarettes and a welcome drink. I tried to imagine what her father might've said to her on the ride to the airport, or the longer flight back to Toronto. But no words would come. It was as if Ingrid's silence had silenced everyone and everything around her.

The traditional overnight sailing trips on Lake Geneva were underway. Pierpont owned a beautiful, poppy-red yacht that slept twelve. Students taking sailing classes got first dibs on the overnights. The rest of the slots were meted out by a Byzantine lottery system that nobody could figure out. It so happened that on our second to last night there, Shirin and I were assigned to the same bunk on the *Gitaine*. (By now, you know that everything at Pierpont was named *gitaine*— the horses, the yacht, even the resident Irish setter that stole our sandals and chewed them to smithereens. Maybe they

thought that by calling everything "gypsy" they could miti-
gate the stuffiness of the place.)

Shirin had been acting increasingly strange since I'd
hypnotized her. Lately, she never seemed to sleep. When I
turned off my bedside lamp, Shirin was wide awake, reading
another one of her gargantuan textbooks. In the morning,
she'd be in the same exact position. I rarely saw her nibble on
anything more than a few pistachios and Gruyère cheese. Her
hip bones started protruding through her pajama bottoms
and her neck looked whittled down, like a desiccated branch.
Sometimes Shirin talked to herself in Farsi. When I tried to
ask her about the Jewish star I'd seen on her gold chain (it'd
since disappeared), she mentioned that her maternal grandmother was half Jewish, but didn't elaborate further.

I wanted to tell her about my father, who'd escaped Poland
during the Warsaw ghetto uprising and had stowed away on a
ship bound for Havana. His journey from Poland across Germany (hiding in barns and garbage dumps) and through war-
torn France (stealing baguettes and cabbages) was the stuff of
family legend. He'd lost his entire family to the concentration
camps.

Every Hanukkah, Papi retold those tales along with the hap-
pier ones that followed in Cuba. Everyone said Max Wahl was
more Cuban than the Cubans, and he became a Cuban citizen
to seal the deal. He learned to speak nearly accentless Spanish
and on the dance floor, he was so silky smooth that he put other
men to shame. In fifteen years, Papi built up the biggest jewelry
empire on the island, took up smoking cigars, and married my
mother—the daughter of a tobacco magnate in Pinar del Río. I
sometimes wondered if Shirin had a similar story to tell.

Shirin didn't want to go on the sailing trip at first, claiming that she was prone to motion sickness. I argued that she hadn't done anything fun all summer, that this would be our last chance to spend time together before going our separate ways. I didn't really expect her to change her mind so I was surprised when she agreed to come.

Downstairs, the shuttle bus was honking impatiently to take us to Lake Geneva. Shirin begged me to go ahead and save her a seat. She needed to pack her bathing suit and promised to come right down. I took her at her word and made the bus wait an extra ten minutes until she arrived, somewhat unsteady and carrying an overnight bag. *Maybe*, I thought, *there might still be a chance to salvage our friendship.*

SHIRIN

On my way down to the bus, I happened to pass the infirmary and found it open and unattended. I walked inside, drawn by the open cabinets stocked with pills. It reminded me of the colorful, tantalizing display of marzipan gnomes at the pastry shop. The same compulsion overtook me. However, this time I did not need to break a window to get what I wanted. I merely reached into the cabinet and helped myself to a handful of yellow-and-green capsules. *Like baby sunflowers*, I thought.

Quickly I turned on the cold water faucet, leaned into the sink, and washed down the capsules in four gulps. Nothing happened, at first—only a lumpy, somewhat bloated feeling in my stomach. Then I hurried down the hallway and out to the courtyard to catch the shuttle bus to the lake. Vivien was glad to see me and patted the free seat next to her. Everyone else seemed irritated by my tardiness. I did not join in the singing or general excitement en route. In fact, I was uncertain why I had agreed to go in the first place. All I wanted was to somehow feel better.

VIVIEN

On the bus to Lake Geneva, a surge of camaraderie infected everyone and we started singing the silly French songs we'd learned in class. My friend Jamila was there, along with Midori, the Japanese girl whom Ingrid had tried to drown. A contingent of gorgeous Scandinavian girls made up the rest of our party.

It was nearly dusk by the time we arrived at the Pierpont yacht, which was magnificent, with masts you had to squint to see to the tops. Madame Godenot was there to see us off. Somehow she didn't seem as forbidding as usual, though her arm muscles were as taut as a sailor's.

The evening was perfect, Caribbean breezy, and we could see the lights of the towns and villages dotting the shores of Lake Geneva. Most of the girls jockeyed for the best seats on deck, wrapping themselves in light sweaters and blankets. The Scandinavians decided to go swimming and dove off the bow, one after another, like a flying fleet of mermaids. I put on my bathing suit and was approaching the guard rail when something made me hesitate.

"Jump!" they hooted at me from the water.

"*Vas-y!*" Midori shouted out with a laugh (nobody had ever heard her laugh before).

I turned to look for Shirin, hoping she might jump with me. The sun was setting and the yacht gleamed with the day's last light. A shiver went through me. That's when I spotted her—huddled in the back of the boat, looking forlornly toward shore. Before I could call out her name, she toppled over into the water like a rag doll, slipping in with barely a splash. If I hadn't been looking for her that very instant, nobody would've seen her fall.

"Shirin!" I screamed. "Girl overboard!" Frantically I pointed to where she'd gone under.

There was mass confusion for what seemed like forever until the Scandinavian girls got it. They swam behind the boat like a school of dolphins and nabbed Shirin as she drifted lifelessly toward the bottom of the lake. They pulled her out of the water, then lifted her up with their bronzed arms up toward the skies like a glorious offering from the goddess of the seas.

DAY
THIRTY

SHIRIN

I was in the hospital for three days. The doctors pumped my stomach and punctured my arms with needles and IVs. It was not Lake Geneva that had nearly killed me, but the pills I had swallowed before going on the yacht. I had not planned this, though it was impossible to convince anyone of the truth.

It turned out that those capsules contained a powerful barbiturate, and that I had taken enough to tranquilize a camel. My father was a heart surgeon—he used to treat the shah and everyone in the royal family for high blood pressure—and he knew as well as anyone what those pills might have done. If Vivien had not noticed me when she did, I would most certainly be dead.

In the hospital, I clung to life for two days before regaining consciousness. When I was finally strong enough, I confessed to the break-in at the pastry shop. It was as if those tranquilizers served as a truth serum, burning through me like a laser. I could not have lied even if I had wanted to. Only Ingrid had suspected me but she told no one. For all her exaggerations, she was an honorable girl. Of course, I felt responsible for her expulsion from Pierpont. I vowed to make amends.

My parents came to collect me in Switzerland. With great sadness, my parents speculated that I might have inherited my maternal grandmother's delicate nervous system. She had been prone to breakdowns and once spent two years in a sanitarium in Baden-Baden. There was no cure for her ailment, the doctors had said, except rest.

CODA

November 11, 1971

Dearest Vivien,

Thank you for your recent letter. You were so kind to write to me after everything that has happened. Please send me your recipes and I will give them to our chef to prepare. I do not have much appetite these days but I promise to try anything you recommend.

I am being treated for depression and anxiety and other unpronounceable disorders. I do not mean to make light of this but to me they are meaningless labels. On the worst days, what I feel is nothing, as if I do not exist. I meet with my psychiatrist daily, a learned man who once studied astronomy and speaks fluent Chinese.

My parents have withdrawn me from school so that I can rest and read at my leisure. Everyone says that I am like my maternal grandmother, oversensitive and high-strung.

She died when I was five so I do not remember her very well.

I do not know what the future will bring, only that I must convince you and Ingrid to give me another chance. I want to invite you both to Tehran for Christmas. Will you please consider this? Will you persuade Ingrid as well? She has not responded to my letters or telegrams.

Please know that I think of you often, and fondly, and cherish the hope that we will see each other again.

Most sincerely,

Shirin

※

January 19, 1972

Dear Ingrid,

Forgive me, but I'm going to skip the niceties. My father has taken a mistress and filed for divorce two days after New Year's. He's moved out and I have no idea where he is. My mother hasn't bothered to get out of bed since he

*left. I'm in a daze. I just keep circling the ice-skating rink
in Central Park, trying to figure out what to do.*

*Last night I found my father's handgun locked away
on the top shelf of his closet. I held it, aimed it at his
photograph on the dresser, felt the cold barrel against
my own cheek. I tried to imagine what it would be like to
catch Papi and his lover in the act. Then I dug into an old
wallet he'd left behind and found a picture of a buxom,
dark-haired woman with a painted-on mole. This was his
new love, the woman he was prepared to ruin his family
over. Why does everything he wants have to hurt us?*

*Sorry to burden you with this but I don't know where else
to turn.*

Love,

Vivien

✳

VIVIEN, LISTEN UP: YOUR DAD IS A COMPLETE ASSHOLE
AND IT'S NOT YOUR FAULT. IF IT WERE ME, I'D SHOOT HIS
BALLS OFF. GET OUT OF THE COLD AND GET ON WITH YOUR
LIFE. HAPPY VALENTINE'S DAY. I MISS YOU. XOXO, INGRID
P.S. MY DAD IS GOING NUTS TOO, BUT IN A DIFFERENT WAY
THAN YOURS. WHEN CAN WE TALK? P.P.S. THAT'S A MOOSE
ON THE OTHER SIDE OF THIS POSTCARD. I DON'T IMAGINE
YOU HAVE THEM IN NYC. HA!

✳

3 MARCH 1972 STOP DEAR INGRID STOP I BEG OF YOU STOP PLEASE RETURN TO PIERPONT THIS SUMMER STOP MY FATHER HAS AGREED TO PAY YOUR TUITION AND TRAVEL STOP EVERYTHING IS ARRANGED STOP THERE IS MUCH TO DISCUSS STOP ALLOW ME TO BEG YOUR FORGIVENESS STOP VIVIEN HAS RECEIVED THE SAME INVITATION STOP THIS IS NOT A JOKE STOP YOU ARE MY ONLY FRIENDS STOP PLEASE SAY YES STOP MOST SINCERELY STOP SHIRIN FIROUZ

"Okay, I know it's April Fools' Day but this can't be for real," Ingrid huffed into the telephone. "I think the princess is going psycho on us again."

"Oh, it's for real all right." Vivien had to raise her voice to be heard over the static of the international call. "Madame Godenot called my dad to tell him about Shirin's father's offer. All expenses paid for both of us. For the whole summer."

"It's seriously weird." Ingrid wasn't convinced. "Her parents must've promised Pierpont a new sailboat, too. Or a science lab, or something for Madame Godenot to get involved. What if Shirin wants us back only to kill us in the middle of the night?"

"Uh, didn't she accuse you of that once?"

"Look, she's been calling here night and day, only I haven't been home. I feel like I'm being fucking stalked." Each time Shirin had telephoned, Ingrid had been out with friends. At least that was what she told her parents. Mostly, she'd been at a motel two towns away with her high school physics teacher, Mr. Drucker, who was married to the English teacher and coached the hockey team on the side. Ingrid wanted to fill Vivien in but it was too complicated a story to tell long distance.

"How bad could it be?" Vivien insisted. "Doesn't everybody deserve a second chance?"

"Oh, what the fuck."

"Then you're in?"

"Yeah, I'm in," Ingrid sighed. "But it's not like I'm joining the goddamn Mouseketeers, or anything. One false move and I'm out of there."

"It's a deal." Vivien laughed.

BOOK TWO:

ARABIAN STALLIONS

SUMMER 1972

DAY
ONE

VIVIEN

I was nervous boarding the plane for Geneva. For one thing, I'd gained fourteen pounds and gone up two dress sizes—without growing so much as an inch. Would anyone even recognize me? My mother tried to console me, saying that it was just a little baby fat and I'd grow out of it. But I don't think you can still have baby fat at fifteen. At fifteen, it's just plain fat. I'd started dressing in what Rena Sherman, a good friend of mine in New York, charitably dubbed "muumuus." She told me that there were lots of guys—"chubby chasers," she called them—who were attracted to zaftig girls. That didn't improve my mood.

Cooking was a bigger passion than ever, and I got bigger along with it. I'd begun teaching myself the ins and outs of French cooking and had worked my way, recipe by recipe, through most of *La Bonne Cuisine* (okay, I skipped over the aspics and lobsters.) Judging by their jacket covers, none of my favorite chefs were sylphs. That didn't console me when I was trying on bathing suits at Lord & Taylor five days before I left for Pierpont. I decided right then that it's psychologically possible to traumatize yourself. I either had to grow eight inches in a huge hurry, or forego eating altogether. The former seemed appealing but unrealistic.

As the plane flew over the pitch-black Atlantic, I thought about everything that had happened the summer before, and since. Would Ingrid and I be able to forge a friendship with Shirin? Maybe I was an idiot, but I wanted to try to fix things. My father used to say that I was like him that way. Wasn't this why he went back to Cuba in the first place—to try to fix things? Instead Papi made a bigger mess than if he hadn't tried at all. I've seen him twice since he left Mom for that other woman, but we didn't have much to say. Correction: He had a lot to say, but I wasn't exactly paying attention.

I pressed my call button and asked the stewardess for a cup of warm milk. When she looked at me strangely, I shrugged and said: "Insomnia." I took a hunk of Belgian chocolate from my purse and dropped it into the milk. My fellow passengers sniffed the air, wondering what the delicious smell was. Before long, those of us in economy rows nineteen and twenty were discussing the varying qualities of international chocolates. Then morning came with its croissants and apricot jam.

At the airport, it was the same orderly chaos at the Pierpont kiosk except that everyone looked a lot younger to me. Maybe I was making a huge mistake. Maybe it was impossible to undo a wrong. Maybe the best anyone could do was forgive and move on. I wanted to forgive my father, but it wasn't so easy. I wanted to give Shirin the benefit of the doubt, too, though I suspected this wouldn't be possible. What was done was done, like a fallen soufflé. All you could do was humbly begin again.

It turned out that I didn't have as much to worry about as I'd feared. Pierpont looked more beautiful than I remembered. There was a welcoming gazebo nestled in the gardens and the dormitory was freshly painted a pale yellow with white trim. It looked like the fantasy castles I'd dreamed of as a girl.

When our bus pulled up to the entrance, Shirin was waiting for me with a huge bouquet of tuberoses, my favorite flower. The smell was overpowering as Shirin embraced me and murmured "Vivi-*joon*," her favorite Farsi term of endearment. She looked so pleased, I thought her face would split in two. This was definitely not the solemn, rigid roommate I remembered.

Shirin had gotten to Pierpont two days before. She led me upstairs to our second-floor room, practically skipping down the wallpapered hallway. First, she'd made certain that we got the biggest suite, then she'd had it professionally decorated. There were fluffy down comforters encased in turquoise silk, matching pillows, and sheer curtains pulled to either side of the picture windows. Not to mention a brand-new stereo and floor-to-ceiling bookshelves.

Shirin opened the biggest steamer trunk I've ever seen, which was entirely filled with presents for Ingrid and me. That was when I started feeling guilty.

"Oh my God, you didn't have to do this," I protested.

This only made Shirin grin harder.

"It was the least I could do after my behavior last summer."

"I liked you fine just the way you were."

"You're lying."

"I swear to God I'm not. You know I love nerds."

Then we got down to the business of catching up. Her year sounded enviable except for the mental breakdown part. She got to skip school, sleep in, read books, and discuss life with some Iranian psychiatrist expert in Chinese philosophy. In the afternoons, she swam in the family pool and got in great shape. *Maybe I should start swimming to trim down*, I thought, but immediately quashed that idea. I hated getting my face wet.

Shirin pinched my arm lovingly and demanded to know what I planned to cook for her this summer.

"All kinds of desserts," I joked but immediately regretted it.

Shirin took it in stride. "Marzipan gnomes, perhaps?"

We both laughed, relieved, and I knew we'd probably be okay.

INGRID

I must've been completely out of my mind to go back to Pierpont. People had accused me of lots of things in my sixteen years, but being a masochist wasn't one of them. I'd pretty much ignored Shirin's entreaties for months. Just because she went insane didn't mean we had to make her feel better about herself. She screwed up. Period. Then she framed me for her crime. So what were we supposed to do now? Sit around holding hands and singing "Kumbaya"?

Besides, I had plenty of my own problems to worry about. Look, if anyone was really losing their marbles, it was my father. On our way home from the Toronto airport last year, about a hundred miles from Wiarton, Vati drove his new station wagon into a ditch. There were no oncoming trucks, no deer jumping into the middle of the road, nothing that would make him swerve the car. I kind of wished there *had* been a real reason instead of Vati's bizarre death wish. The only ones hurt were us: nine nasty bruises between Kathe and me, and another lump on our dad's head.

His war memories got worse after that second accident. Vati woke up in cold sweats, reliving every harrowing hour with the Nazis. It turned out that he'd participated in his share of brutal deeds, too, including the suppression of the Warsaw ghetto uprising. We'd read about it in history class. It made me ashamed to be German. It didn't help that the teacher kept looking at me every time he uttered the word *Nazi*. Like I was responsible for the psychosis of an entire generation of Germans.

One night at dinner, I asked Vati how many people he thought he'd killed during World War II. My mother looked at me aghast, as if I'd threatened them both with a butcher knife. My father turned pale and ran to the guest bathroom, where he got sick for the rest of the evening.

Anyway, it wasn't until Vivien called me that spring and begged me to reconsider that I decided to give Pierpont and the Iranian princess another try. What did I have to lose? I certainly didn't need to hang around rural Ontario and entertain the farm boys. That physics teacher turned out to be bad news, too. When he brought a rope to our latest rendezvous and begged me to tie him up, I knew it would be our last.

I wasn't inclined to continue driving Vati to the nether

reaches of Canada to sell his fans either. At my mother's pleading, I'd already spent most of my March break doing just that. It might've been fun—I loved being on the open road—except for Vati's ridiculous sales pitches. At one dry goods store in Saskatchewan, he threw a model fan on the floor and stomped on it like a chimpanzee. To demonstrate its sturdiness, he said.

So when Vivien pressed me to return to Pierpont, I relented. Besides, maybe I'd run into that hunk of a Russian wrestler again. Next time I wouldn't waste time with small talk. That was going to be my new motto: *No more small talk.*

My sister didn't come along to Switzerland that year. I didn't know how she managed it but she became, seemingly overnight, an internationally ranked tennis player. Kathe convinced our parents to send her to some junior Wimbledon camp in England. The Canadian dollar was pretty strong against European currencies in those days so it was cheaper to send us abroad than to keep us home. The real deal, though, was that they were exhausted and welcomed the chance to send us as far away as possible.

On the flight to Geneva, I got to talking with Mr. Crewcut in the seat across from me. It turned out he was some kind of crazy youth preacher on an international mission. He tried proselytizing me with a fistful of Christian pamphlets and his eerie, wanna-hypnotize-you blue eyes. I held my palm out in front of his face like a traffic cop and said: "No more. Do you hear me, you little Jesus freak?" I would've pushed him out the emergency exit but I didn't want to get the summer off to a bad start.

The Pierpont Boarding School for Girls was just as I

remembered it. Not a leaf out of place. The same stupid Greek goddesses fountain burbling in the garden. The same spoiled-to-death, designer-clad, tittering half-wits running around all over the place. This was a megamistake. As I was considering hitchhiking back to the airport for a flight to Timbuktu, I saw them: Vivien and Shirin, standing on the front steps waiting for me. They screamed so loud and happily that damned if they didn't get me a little choked up.

Let's just say it took a lot to shock me. Not to sound arrogant or anything, but I was usually the one doing the shocking. Try to imagine how bug-eyed I got when Vivien and the princess dragged me to our room, banged open the door, and shouted: "Surprise!" The place looked like a luxury hotel room, or something out of *Arabian Nights*. What I said to them was: "Shit, is this where the harem sleeps, or what?" They thought that was the most hilarious thing they'd ever heard. The more I stood there staring at their exhilarated, distorted faces, the more nervous I got.

I was in definite need of a cigarette and pulled a pack out of my knapsack, offering them each a Marlboro. For a few minutes, we stood there smoking and smiling at each other like a trio of baboons, glad to be in one another's company. I took a deep breath. Okay, maybe this wasn't going to be so bad after all.

My complacency was abruptly shattered when Shirin started pulling luxury items out of her leather trunk. We're talking serious jewelry. We're talking velvet-lined boxes filled with gold bracelets and rings. We're talking Hermés scarves and Gucci accessories—wallets, key chains, monogrammed purses. We're talking fancy Swiss watches that told time in the outer reaches of the planetary system. We're talking all this for Vivien and me. I thought our princess had gone off an even deeper end than I'd imagined.

SHIRIN

As much as I thought I had disliked the experience of our first summer together, I looked back on those weeks with what I could only describe as a fond nostalgia. It was a funny idea, nostalgia. It made me think of old people reminiscing about their youth, or an exile looking longingly back at his homeland, regardless of how oppressive it might have been. For me, the nostalgia was not for what *was*, but for what could have been. That first summer in Switzerland, I had remained hidden behind my mathematics textbooks, refusing to engage with Vivien, or Ingrid, or any of the other girls. I had adamantly refused to participate in my own life.

Vivien and Ingrid were stunned when they walked into our new room. You could very nearly see their minds at work, translating everything into monetary terms. This must have cost that. That must have cost this. Dollar signs everywhere. But that was not how we did things in my country. In my country, the grand gesture is everything. Nobody goes around examining the price tags. Even the lowliest nomads in the desert are inclined to extravagance, given half a chance. What I most desired was to demonstrate, in no uncertain terms, how much I cared about them.

"This is my way of saying 'I'm sorry,'" I said. "My behavior last summer was inexcusable. Please forgive me."

"You're making way too much of this, Princess," Ingrid said. "Ancient history."

"Really, Shirin, this is so unnecessary," Vivien added kindly.

She seemed more open than Ingrid, who looked embarrassed and uncomfortable. An essential optimism like Vivien's was something I fought to maintain every day. I suspected that Ingrid and I were forged of more cynical mettle—for different reasons. Perhaps my suspicion of strangers, the inbred expectation that things would go wrong or that people you did not know would try to cheat you, came from centuries of tribalism. A personal enemy became your family's enemy for life. And the fighting did not end in heaven.

My coup de grâce came the first evening of our reunion, after dinner. I arranged for the three of us to be driven to the equestrian center near Rolle. Predictably, neither Ingrid nor Vivien had signed up for horseback riding that summer. Vivien had given up riding after her experience with Pierpont's unspectacular equines the year before. And Ingrid claimed that she had enough trouble with bipeds without complicating her life with four-legged creatures.

However, I had something unusual waiting for them.

We approached the outdoor riding ring. The summer dusk lingered forever, suffusing my three Arabian stallions with a burnished light. Even from a distance, it was obvious these were no ordinary beasts.

"Oh, look," Vivien said, pointing to the prize-winning specimens from my father's stables. "They finally got some decent horses. Let's hope they're not all named Gitaine this time."

"Whoa, they look like mythological beasts." Ingrid whistled. "They're perfect. Perfection. Überperfection. What the hell are they doing at Pierpont?"

Then she looked at me, and she knew.

"These are *your* horses?"

"Not my horses. *Our* horses."

"What?!" Vivien shrieked, startling the beasts, which began snorting and cantering around the ring.

"No way," Ingrid whispered. She could not take her eyes off them.

"Do you like them?" I asked.

Ingrid's mouth dropped. For once, she had nothing to say.

Vivien's questions came fast and furiously. "What are they doing here? How did you bring them over? Do we get to ride them?" Her hands clenched and released, as if she were kneading dough.

"Yes, I had them brought over for us," I measured my words carefully. "So that we could ride them together this summer."

"What happened to the old horses?" Vivien asked.

"They're still here. But I could not abide those tired hags any longer."

Ingrid still had not said anything, only stared at the horses. The trio of stallions was standing together now, muzzles facing each other, like the spokes of a wheel. There was no denying their resplendence.

"Is this okay?" I asked Ingrid. "You are not offended?"

She looked at me incredulously. "I've never seen more beautiful animals in my life."

"Do you want to ride them? I could—"

"Are they safe?" Vivien interrupted.

"Yes," I said. "But they are fast. Very fast."

"I want to ride them," Ingrid said. There was no trace of her usual snideness. "When can we ride them?"

"Right now," I said. "Follow me."

I led them to the edge of the ring and opened the gate. I cooed their names: Bahman, Asad, and Cyrus, after my brothers. The horses were a bit skittish from their journey. My father had sent them by ship via the Persian Gulf and the Arabian and Red Seas, then through the Suez Canal, across the Mediterranean, and up along the western coast of Italy to the French Riviera. From there, they had boarded a specially equipped truck for the long drive to Switzerland.

Maybe the horses missed the scent of the desert, like me. Maybe they longed for the sounds of a familiar language, a particular quality of oats, the compact weight of my father on their bare backs. I had ridden each of the horses the day before to soothe them. They had grown calmer but were not yet themselves.

"Come here, my darlings," I murmured to them in Farsi. "You are my sweet boys." I pulled apples and carrots from my satchel and let them eat. Their appetites were not one hundred percent.

Vivien and Ingrid watched me with fascination. I motioned for them to enter the ring. They approached cautiously, accepting the supply of sugar cubes I gave them to feed the horses. Cyrus took to Ingrid immediately, and Vivien tried to bond with Asad. I went to the stalls and came back with reins, a mounting ladder, fluorescent helmets, and three pairs of new calfskin riding boots.

Vivien put her boots on first. "Jeez, these are like . . ."

"Butter?" Ingrid offered as she pulled on hers.

"We are going to ride them bareback," I announced.

"You're kidding me." Vivien flinched but Ingrid was intrigued.

"That is the best way to ride them," I explained, as I put the reins on the horses and adjusted their silver-plated bits. "They were specially trained for this. Besides, at the speeds they go, you need to be fused to their backs or you will fall off. They are not accustomed to saddles so the chances of them bucking you would be exponentially higher."

"Bu-bucked?" Vivien stammered, trying to center her helmet on her head.

"It may happen sometime. What you need to remember is to tuck your body in like a baby in the . . . what do you call it?"

"Fetal position?" Ingrid was supplying all the missing words today.

"Womb?" Vivien suggested.

"Yes, that is it. And protect your head at all costs. You can recover from almost anything except a head injury."

"Why are these so bright?" Vivien pointed to her helmet. "You could spot them in outer space."

"That is precisely the point. If you are lost in the desert and your horse has run off, they will send aircraft to find you. Bright pink stands out in the desert."

"That's intense," Ingrid said.

"Who wants to go?" I asked.

"Why don't you show us first?" Vivien insisted.

I slipped onto Bahman's back and stood there, letting them take in the beauty of their first mounted Arabian stallion.

"Wow . . . ," they said in unison. This was highly unusual. Ingrid and Vivien never said anything in unison.

"Another very important thing. Do not perform any sudden or harsh movements. You need to treat them with the utmost gentleness in word and deed. Arabians are not like other horses. You do not need to kick or whip them. The slightest suggestion will do. They are exquisitely sensitive. Any questions?"

Vivien and Ingrid shook their heads, again in unison. I clicked my tongue, squeezing my thighs against Bahman's flanks. I had him go in a slow trot along the periphery of the corral. The other two horses followed suit. As I said, they were extraordinarily well-trained.

My roommates were in the middle of the ring, watching us go round and round.

"Are you ready?" I asked, stopping.

"Yes," they said, ever in lockstep.

I dismounted and commanded the horses to wait, which they did.

"Who's first?"

My roommates looked at each other and, by some unspoken agreement, Ingrid stepped forward. She was surprisingly graceful mounting Cyrus. Her posture was perfect, her stance relaxed and in control simultaneously. I could not believe that she had never been on a horse. I did not think that Cyrus, if he could talk, would imagine that he had anything but an expert rider on his back.

"Just walk him until I get Vivien ready," I instructed, and Ingrid did just that. She was the most natural rider I had ever seen.

Poor Vivien was another story. I do not know whether it was the extra weight, or her anxious temperament, but she was frightfully ungainly. She scrambled onto Asad's back then lay flat forward, grabbing his neck for dear life. Her buttocks protruded in the air like a hillock. Asad, the finest horse in Baba's entire stable, stared at me as if to say: *What in the name of Allah are you doing to me?*

My father maintained that you could tell everything about a person by watching them ride a horse: whether they are honest or gracious, mean-spirited, or a common crook. Baba never did serious business with anyone without first taking them for a ride. It did not matter how long or expertly they had ridden, either. The evidence, Baba said, was in how they treated their horse. Looking at Vivien and Ingrid, I would have to conclude that both were good-hearted girls.

"Can we leave the ring?" Ingrid called out.

Everyone was composed—even Vivien was finding her stride—and so I thought it acceptable to ride in the woods for a short while.

"Follow me." I opened the gate for our horses to pass.

Everything went splendidly for the first twenty minutes or so. We proceeded along an easy trail in the woods. The forest birds were flitting about, trying to secure their last meals of the day. The earth smelled damp and rich with decay. It was getting chilly but the heat of the horses warmed us.

We kept a steady pace. I did not want to risk anything going wrong on our first outing. Ingrid heard the water first, a stream swollen by the recent rains. Although Arabians can go many miles without water, I encouraged our horses to stop and drink. It was an idyllic evening. My hope of returning to Switzerland and befriending my old roommates had come to pass. They were with me, and I had done something to please them.

I could not have expected what happened next.

One minute, Asad was contentedly drinking his fill from the stream. The next, he shot like an arrow into the forest. I heard Vivien's screams and the crash of breaking branches and knew she had fallen. When I found her a hundred yards ahead, she was crumpled at the foot of a pine tree. Her arm was bent at an impossible angle, the elbow jutting into her ribs. I jumped off my horse and went to her, taking her hand in mine. She was deathly pale and her breathing was shallow. She needed to get to a hospital immediately.

Ingrid galloped up on Cyrus, and stopped next to me.

"Holy shit! Are you all right?"

But Vivien closed her eyes and slumped to the ground, unconscious.

DAY
THREE

VIVIEN

I didn't know that pain could generate so many colors and smells. This was my first thought when I woke up in the Catholic hospital in Lausanne. The pain in my broken elbow was a ferocious red with flecks of yellow, like floating bits of fat. My fractured rib was a dark forest green. Maybe it was the sight of those nuns in their old-fashioned habits that got me hallucinating. Or maybe the parts of my brain that controlled color and pain had crossed wires somehow. Regardless, it was seriously strange. Everything I saw, heard, tasted, and smelled automatically got translated into colors.

To me, the hospital reeked of purplish boiled cabbage and my attending physician, the fastidious Dr. Gilbert Moireaux, was a faded coral with striations of burnt umber. None of this worried me except for the fact that it might screw up my cooking. What if my soufflés suddenly looked blue or smelled like cat food? When I told Ingrid and Shirin about my symptoms—they came to visit me every day after morning French classes—they were equally puzzled.

Finally, Dr. Moireaux pronounced that I was likely suffering from a rare case of temporary synesthesia. Or, at least he thought it was temporary.

"What color am I?" Ingrid demanded when she learned of my diagnosis.

"A mixture of brilliant blues and greens, like peacock feathers."

"You gotta love this disorder." She laughed. "But aren't there a bunch of evil eyes on those feathers?"

"As a matter of fact, there are," Shirin said glumly.

"What about the princess here? What color is she?"

"Truly, I would rather not know."

"Come on, Shirin. Let's make a rainbow together," Ingrid joked.

I looked at Shirin and she shrugged at me noncommittally. I knew she felt terrible about what had happened. It wasn't her fault. I'd told her this a million times but she still felt responsible.

"Shirin is . . . well, Shirin is pure gold." It was kind of embarrassing to say this but it was true. She shone like one of those Academy Awards statues.

"Please excuse me," Shirin said and hurried out of the room.

"Did you see that?" Ingrid said with amazement. "I think you actually made her cry."

I lay back on my pillows and took a deep breath, though

it hurt my ribs. To my surprise, Ingrid began smoothing my blanket and fluffing my pillows. She poured me a fresh glass of water and snuck in a stack of gossip magazines from the waiting room.

"Who knew you were a nursemaid at heart?" I teased her.

"Yeah, a regular Clara Barton," Ingrid sniped. "Look, I could break you out of here if you wanted me to."

How she got her trusty toolbox past security was one of her many unheralded gifts. Ingrid brandished an enormous saw and eyed the bars of my hospital window. I tried to dissuade her from doing anything drastic.

"You're no fun at all," Ingrid said and put the saw away.

"Hey, maybe you should go find Shirin. She's going to be hospitalized for guilt if she doesn't stop soon."

"Any more breast beating and she'll break her own ribs."

Ingrid and I laughed. It felt good to laugh, even through the pain. Then she grew serious.

"Look, I don't know about you but I'm really uncomfortable with the whole laying-on-of-the-gifts deal. It's so outrageous. I know her family is filthy rich, but this is way over the top."

"I think she meant well."

"I'm not saying she didn't. It's not like she's lording it over us or anything. And God knows those horses are fucking amazing. For all we know, this is small potatoes in her world, but—"

"But what?"

"I think she's trying to buy our friendship somehow." Ingrid cracked her knuckles. "Look, first she showers us with gifts, then—"

"That's crazy."

"Something's definitely wrong. She in no way resembles the person who shared our room last summer."

"She's changed, Ingrid. She spent a year swimming and reading and going to a shrink and maybe she's realized that—"

"What? That she wants to make friends with us commoners?"

That made me laugh again, and I held on to my ribs with my good arm. "I'd hardly call you common."

"You know what I mean."

"Maybe she loves us. Is that such a crime?"

"Love is always a crime."

"Cynic."

"Romantic."

"Shh, here she comes."

Shirin returned from the bathroom with her eyes red and swollen. Ingrid was right. It was hard to believe that she was the same emotionless girl from our first summer together. That girl saw everything through the cold, clear lens of scientific inquiry. That girl avoided the messy interactions of teenagers, preferring to stick to the stark beauty of a perfect equation. That girl was an unequivocal snob. The girl in front of me, twelve months later, was another person altogether, someone I was curious to get to know.

"Enough with the waterworks already," Ingrid said. "If you don't cut it out, you're going to have to switch places with Vivien here. Or worse yet, we'll have to cart you off to where the patients wear straitjackets. Is that what you want?"

Shirin tried to smile. I patted the bed and beckoned her

over. "The food sucks here but it beats having to conjugate French verbs at the crack of dawn."

"Speaking of . . ." Ingrid pulled out her French grammar book and started reciting in a fake professorial voice: *"Je monterai, tu monteras, il/elle montera, nous monterons, vous monterez."* She stopped and looked up at us with an evil grin. "I'm just trying to be encouraging."

We continued with other declensions of "to ride." Past perfect: "She had ridden." Simple preterit: "Once she rode and then she rode no more." The ever impossible subjunctive: "I wish I could ride again." The nonnegotiable imperative: "We *will* ride again." Shirin got first prize for the toughest conjugation of all—future perfect continuous: "I will have been riding." As in: "By the end of July, I will have been riding one of the finest horses on this unholy planet for almost a month."

Wishful thinking, that one. Even though I told my roommates that I'd be willing to get back on a horse once I felt better, I had no intention of doing so. The kitchen was a lot safer than the back of a thousand-pound beast. I didn't want to make Shirin feel worse so I kept my mouth shut. Besides, there was next to no chance that Dr. Moireaux or the gatekeepers at Pierpont would let me go riding, in any case.

Actually, I liked lying in bed all day and being waited on hand and foot. For once, the attention was focused on me. With the food so dreadful and my resulting loss of appetite, I was also losing weight like crazy. Mostly, I relished the chance to do nothing but luxuriate and read. That summer I was tackling Dostoevsky, specifically, *The Brothers Karamazov*. His descriptions of Russians made Cubans look like wallflowers.

Anyway, if it weren't for the inedible meals and the crazy color hallucinations, I would've been happy to stay in the hospital for months.

Soon enough, though, I was back at Pierpont with only a few restrictions on my activities. Above all, no heavy lifting in cooking class. Another instructor had replaced Chef d'Aubigné, who'd been fired during the winter session for smacking a Sicilian girl on her bottom with a wooden spoon. It was meant to be playful, I'm sure, but when her father, Don Giordano Buccellato of Palermo, heard about it, he gave the headmistress two choices: get rid of the chef, or he'd do it for them (permanently). That was what everyone said, anyway. At Pierpont, rumors always trumped the truth.

My family freaked out when they heard about my accident. Mami and Tía Cuca threatened to get on a plane and bring me home, but I convinced them not to come. My father called out of the blue, though we weren't officially on speaking terms. He was in a remote diamond mining town in the Congo and had to shout into the phone for me to hear him. Papi promised to visit me in Switzerland en route to New York. He said he had a surprise for me, though I didn't necessarily take that as good news. His surprises too often turned out to be disasters.

I didn't tell anyone he was coming, I'm not sure why. Maybe I wanted to preserve something that was just ours, like the times we used to go to the shooting range in Miami behind my mother's back. Or maybe I was trying to decide whether I could forgive him, and I didn't want someone else's opinion to influence me.

DAY SEVEN

INGRID

Another Saturday night and I was, predictably, the goddamn social director again. Why did everyone look to me for entertainment? Did I look like Johnny Carson? It made me wonder what people did when I wasn't around. Sit around and watch reruns of *The Brady Bunch*? Pathetic. I shouldn't have bothered to get the troops ready for another dance with Le Rosey. Call it sick loyalty. Call it perversity. Call it an irresistible challenge. Whatever. But duty called and hey, I answered the call.

I thought things could be different this summer. There were a few repeat campers from the year before but mostly I had a fresh crop of girls to work with. They'd heard just enough about me to be both intrigued and intimidated. It wasn't every day that someone got kicked out of Pierpont for alleged crimi-

nal activity and then was personally begged by the headmistress to return the following year. I guess it wasn't the worst
reputation I could've gotten.

I spent the two days prior to the dance consulting on ward-
robes and dispensing sexual advice. There may have been
other girls who'd already slept with boys but they wouldn't
have admitted it. It wasn't cool to say you'd done it, even if
you had. Believe me, even in so-called artistic circles, this
was the fast track to slutdom. But what did I care? I didn't go
to the trouble of sleeping with five guys in a year to forego
bragging rights. Most of the time, the sex was worthless. Boys
my age were in it for themselves and didn't have a clue about
female anatomy. I was better off taking care of myself. For
shock-value fun, I showed some wide-eyed fourteen-year-
olds how to give a blow job on a banana. When I finished, I
peeled it and ate it in three tidy bites.

The big excitement that first Saturday in July was that the
dance—costumes optional—would be held at Le Rosey for a
change. We'd heard about its storied grounds, the princely
dining halls, its polo ponies, and Adonis tennis instructors.
Le Rosey's roster of famous alumni now ruled the world. But,
frankly, I was primarily interested in finding myself a halfway decent boyfriend for the summer.

Thanks to Shirin and her magic, bottomless steamer
trunk, our crowd was dressed to the nines. Against my
advice, Vivien wore an unflattering lavender belly dancing
outfit complete with ankle bracelets and finger cymbals. Plus
Shirin glued glitter on Vivien's pudgy stomach. Sure, she'd
lost a lot of weight in the hospital but this was hardly figure
enhancing. I think that fall off the horse did more than make

her dizzy for the color wheel. The girl lost her mind and her fashion sense simultaneously.

Shirin decided to wear her English riding outfit and brought along her crop, which she periodically snapped against her thigh. "To keep the boys in line," she said with a laugh. Whoa, with that kind of competition, I definitely needed to up the ante. Thank God for thrift stores. After extensive deliberations, I donned a gold lamé minidress that I paired with fishnet stockings and black patent dominatrix boots. I thought of bringing along a gleaming steel hammer (I kept a spare in my toolbox) but I didn't want to scare off the pretty boys. My makeup was pure sixties—pale white lipstick and enough eyeliner for a remake of *Cleopatra*. When we strode up to the shuttle bus that was taking us to the party, all conversation stopped. It was like the Mod Squad had arrived. Oh yeah, we were hot.

The reaction at Le Rosey was even more dramatic: open-mouthed gaping followed by the jostling of horny boys looking for a mate. A tall blond boy with a crooked jumble of teeth made a beeline for Shirin. *Good for her,* I thought. The orthodontics could come later. I glanced around to see if, by some remote chance, my ever-elusive Russian wrestler was on hand. No luck. Undeterred, I searched for the next best candidate. Shyly hovering near a rose bush was the second most handsome boy I'd ever seen: a luxuriantly tall, olive-skinned, thick-haired beauty with the most luscious lips to be found on any testosterone-saturated creature this side of the moon. He was so blazingly gorgeous it almost hurt to look at him.

But wait. This god on earth, Mr. Perfection Incarnate,

made a jaw-dropping beeline for Vivien—Vivien!—and said loud enough for everyone to hear: "I was so hoping to see you again."

What?!

VIVIEN

I'm glad he recognized me because I wouldn't have recognized *him* in a million years. When he came over to me, took my hands in his, and stared at me with his brown-bordering-on-hazel eyes, I was struck dumb. He was hoping to see *me* again? Who was *he*? Everyone was watching us and I could feel Ingrid's laser stare boring into the side of my skull. I started panicking, wondering what I was supposed to do. Then I felt his warm, meaty hands sweating over mine and I remembered—or rather, my body remembered. It was Omar, a remote version of the Omar I remembered from the year before. Except that now he looked like the previous Omar's gorgeous older brother.

I, on the other hand, *looked more beautiful than ever.* Those were his exact words. American boys could never say something like that with a straight face.

"Please, come with me," Omar insisted.

By then my hands were sweating, too, and we were dripping with mutual recognition. I had no choice. I followed him in the flimsy belly dancing outfit that I shouldn't have let Shirin convince me to wear. Omar was careful to take my good arm. The other was still wrapped in a bulky white elbow cast.

"You will have to tell me the story of your arm."

Indeed.

Omar led me to a table in Le Rosey's extensive gardens. The party was in full swing. Pretty Chinese lanterns hung everywhere and the scent of lilies and flowering vines perfumed the air. The colors were overwhelming, like I was inside a washing machine on the fast cycle. Uniformed waiters served hors d'oeuvres and sparkling cider on silver trays. Omar noticed me eyeing the hors d'oeuvres (I hadn't eaten beforehand, conscious of my bare midriff) and called over the waiter.

"Two of everything, please," he ordered. His voice sounded intensely violet to me, the kind of violet you see at the edge of sunsets.

I was grateful for Omar's attentiveness because I was immensely hungry. I dove into an endive leaf spread with aged Roquefort cheese. *When in doubt,* I thought, *eat.* When in abject fear of making a fool of yourself, eat. When an insanely seductive boy paid attention to you, eat. Basically, it was my solution to everything. I tried a square of asparagus quiche followed by triangles of foie gras and crunchy cornichons.

Omar watched me eat and smiled, like he'd never enjoyed anything more. The fact is, he was looking a little nervous himself. His right hand left a stain on the linen that was a dead ringer for Michigan.

"Aren't you going to try anything?" I mumbled, my mouth half full. "This is wonderful. I've been living on hospital food for days. It's like being released from prison."

Suddenly, I realized I was talking too much. Way too much. Why couldn't I simply mimic his sweet economy of words? Maybe if I kept eating, I would say less. A lot less. That, at least, was my hope.

"Hospital?" He had a look of pure, adorable concern. I

didn't know whether it was him or the superb hors d'oeuvres but I was on the verge of swooning like some 1940s actress. Could this really be happening to me?

"I'll tell you about it sometime." I shrugged, not wanting to get into the details of my ejection from Shirin's horse. "But it involves an Arabian stallion named Asad and an anonymous woodland creature."

"You mean, like a fox?"

"Perhaps."

"Or a weasel?"

"Could be."

"Ah, a woman of mystery. I love that." Omar took my undamaged arm again just as I was reaching for a baked sausage puff. "You have no idea how often I've thought of you this past year. When you didn't show up to the last dance, I was, uh, heartbroken."

"Heartbroken?" I was eating so fast that I started choking.

"Yes, I vowed that if I ever had the privilege of seeing you again, I would not hesitate to tell you."

"Uh, okay." I gulped some sparkling cider.

"I hope I'm not embarrassing you." He looked down and his eyelashes practically grazed his cheeks. There was no denying it. The boy was beautiful.

"No, it's not that. It's just that . . . this is so sudden and . . . unexpected."

"Please forgive my precipitousness." I watched his lips as he said "precipitousness." The coming together and pulling apart of those delectable pillows of flesh. I tried to regain my composure and take in his whole face. It was a study in contrition. Then it was my turn to speak.

"Um, well, don't take this the wrong way or anything but you've, uh, changed. A lot, I mean." This wasn't going well. The more I said, the worse it got. If only he would let go of my hand, I could try one of those miniature raspberry tartlets and feel better. When dementedly attracted to the most unassuming poster boy of the century but terrified of screwing up, eat. Eat, eat, eat.

"Everyone in my family is very tall," he said apologetically.

"Oh, no, I didn't mean that in a bad way!"

"My mother was concerned that I would stay short forever. But then I had what they call a 'growth spurt,' and everything changed."

You're telling me, I wanted to say, but I didn't.

Omar paused, looking distraught. "My voice, my hands, everything is different. I hope these changes are not distasteful to you."

"No, I wouldn't say that." I managed to tug my hand free. This stunning boy was practically declaring his love for me and all I wanted to do was run for my life. I needed time to regroup. To get Ingrid's advice. Immediately.

Omar's face softened and he raised his glass of cider. I picked mine up, too, to be polite.

"To seeing you again," he offered a toast. "You are even lovelier than I remember. More beautiful than my every dream of you."

"Uh, same here," I said, and we clinked glasses.

DAY
ELEVEN

SHIRIN

From one day to the next, I had a boyfriend. Certainly, I was the last person to expect this turn of events. His name was Jan-Peter von Schoonhoven and he was from the Netherlands, spoke six languages, played the flute, and was an expert equestrian. We met the moment I arrived at Le Rosey. Or, rather, he singled me out and came right over and introduced himself. Jan-Peter told me that he was drawn to my riding outfit and my defiant stance, that he could tell by looking at me that I was very intelligent. Somehow I felt *recognized*, as if nobody before him (except for my brother, Cyrus) had ever seen me before. I had not realized until then how invisible I felt.

Naturally, I missed everything else that transpired that evening. Ingrid was flabbergasted that only she, of the three of us, did not "snag," as she so delicately put it, a "hunk" for the night.

Not that Jan-Peter was conventionally handsome. He was tall and bony and his front teeth overlapped in a funny way. But his eyes, a soft gray, anchored everything into place. I was surprised by the sudden ferocity of my feelings for him. I had assumed that I was immune to the vicissitudes of romantic love, especially after what had happened with that degenerate last year. When my cousins in Tehran spoke of their exuberant admiration for this boy or that, I thought them fools.

That summer, I became the fool.

Ingrid was irritable for days, accusing Vivien and me of abandoning our friendship in the "tawdry pursuit of the opposite sex." While she freely advised everyone else on how to handle boys, Ingrid was mum on the subject when it came to us. She would light a cigarette, blow smoke out the window, and haughtily pronounce: "You'll just have to find out for yourselves, won't you?"

Her attitude, in my opinion, was unwarranted. Vivien and I discussed it at length but we could not decide whether Ingrid was jealous (unlikely, since she could have had her pick of boys), incredulous (possible, since neither Vivien nor I had had boyfriends before), concerned (also possible, given our inexperience), or hormonally imbalanced (this was Vivien's theory but I found it sexist and refused to subscribe to it).

One thing we could both agree on: It was decidedly unpleasant.

That Wednesday after lunch, we approached Ingrid again. She was fussing with her tools, building some kind of bird house for fledgling sparrows. You never knew what to expect with Ingrid. One minute, she could be sawing the locks off Pierpont's freezers; the next, providing shelter for the homeless birds of Switzerland.

"Don't get mad at us, but we really need to talk to you," Vivien said. "We're having romantic crises here and we don't have anyone to turn to for advice."

"Forget it, ladies. The love guru is not available." Ingrid kept hammering away at the bird house.

"Look, we heard about your, uh, demonstration on the banana to the younger girls. It's only fair that you share your—"

"Specialized knowledge?" I offered.

"Yeah, that's right, specialized knowledge," Vivien said. "With the two people at Pierpont who care about you the most. Why are you holding out on us, anyway? Did we do something to hurt your feelings?"

" . . . "

"This is embarrassing for me to admit," I said. "But I think I may be in love."

"Me, too," Vivien said. "I mean, I'm not sure I'm in love, but whatever it is, I'm really scared and need to know what to do next."

"You're barking up the wrong tree, ladies." Ingrid wasn't budging but at least she put her hammer down. This was progress, of sorts.

"Would you kindly desist from calling us 'ladies'?" I insisted.

"What would you prefer? 'Traitors'?"

"That is entirely uncalled for."

"Can we get beyond this, please?" Vivien whined.

"As I started to say," Ingrid said, ostentatiously clearing

her throat, "I'm no expert on love. In fact, I disapprove of it. Too messy, entangling, a recipe for heartbreak. Women always get the short end of *that* stick."

"So what are you an expert in?" Vivien demanded.

"Sex."

"Sex?" Vivien and I asked simultaneously.

"A veteran of all-the-way but a world-class expert in blow jobs. So you see, ladies, I cannot help you with your dilemmas."

"What about kissing?" Vivien was not giving up.

"Well, yes, a certain amount of that is usually involved."

"Could you show us how to do it?" I asked tentatively.

"You seemed to be doing just fine at the garden party, Princess."

"I did not like it very much but I want to like it."

"Can you help us like it?" Vivien insisted.

"Maybe you two are lesbians. You should practice together."

Vivien and I looked at each other, eyes wide, then back at Ingrid.

"You mean, you've never practiced kissing with other girls?"

"Uh, no," Vivien said.

"Me neither."

"Who wants to go first?" Ingrid clapped her hands together, all business.

"You can't be serious." Vivien sounded nervous.

"Why not?" Ingrid puckered up.

"I will try." I closed my eyes and felt the warmth of Ingrid's face approaching mine. Then her lips, soft and insistent, pressed against my mouth. At least there were no scratchy bristles to contend with. After a moment, I felt her pull away.

"You've got to open your mouth, Princess. It feels like you have goddam lockjaw."

Vivien was hovering close by, watching our every move, imitating us silently, like a pale pantomime.

Dutifully, I opened my mouth.

"Cut the blowfish act, for God's sake. You've got to open just slightly. This way your shining knight can slip his tongue between your lips and root around."

"That seems superunsanitary," Vivien said.

"Dog saliva is cleaner but do you want to be kissing dogs?"

Vivien and I laughed nervously then I returned to the task at hand. Ingrid showed me how to accommodate a boy's tongue and lightly flick one's own in a sexy, encouraging manner, run it along his teeth. ("Not like you're hoisting a flag up a pole, okay?") When we were done, I wiped my mouth, which was producing excess saliva. It was not as bad as I had feared. The worst part was Ingrid's stale tobacco taste but I wanted to avoid inciting her wrath further and did not mention it. That summer, I tried to give up smoking in the name of kissing Jan-Peter.

"What about you, Vivien?"

"Nah, I think I got it. Thanks."

"You don't want to lose a boy over being an inept kisser, do you?"

"Did we just French kiss?" I asked.

"Not exactly. That's a lot more involved. More involved than I want to get with either of you, anyway. No, we just did Kissing 101. French kissing is more . . . muscular. Your tongues are basically in a wrestling match. Whoever gets to the other's throat first wins."

"That's disgusting." Vivien made a face.

"What can I say? Love isn't for the fainthearted."

"You mean sex, don't you?" Vivien asked.

"I guess I mean either one."

After our kissing lesson, I felt strange and unsettled but also better prepared for my next encounter with Jan-Peter. He had called me the night before to make plans for the weekend. He wanted to go horseback riding and promised that he knew a wonderful trail through the mountains. I had not told Jan-Peter about my Arabians lodged for the summer at the Pierpont stalls. I thought it best to wait. First I wanted to watch him ride and see what kind of boy he was, what kind of man he might become.

"I have an idea," I said.

"I hope you don't think I'm going to be profligate with these kissing sessions, Princess."

"*Merci*, Ingrid, but I think I have enough to go on for now. What I am thinking about is a much grander adventure."

"Than kissing me? I'm terribly hurt."

"Please, can we go riding again?" I looked at my room-mates expectantly.

"Uh, uh . . . I'm still . . ." Vivien looked nervous.

"Scared out of your wits?" Ingrid joked.

"Basically."

"I will be exceedingly careful next time," I said. "I give you my word."

DAY FIFTEEN

INGRID

The world as I knew it was topsy-turvy. My two roommates had found boyfriends the first week at camp—not fly-by-night, meaningless, quickie encounters, either. They were in love, and I, for one, found them annoying as hell. Why did lovebirds have to nauseate everyone around them? I'd read somewhere that to the brain, love and madness were one and the same. For starters, all rational thought flew out the window. Obsessive behavior eclipsed everything else, like sleeping and eating. In short, love managed to put even basic survival instincts on hold.

Conclusion: To be in love is to be temporarily insane. So why did I want a piece of it, too?

Maybe I was too cynical to fall in love. Maybe I saw boys for who they really were: derelict sacks of self-centered, raging hormones. Maybe there were other kinds of boys out there but I seemed to attract only the selfish ones. Maybe it wouldn't have been so dismal if I hadn't spotted Omar first and thought, *Hmm, that guy's hot.* It was painful to watch him enraptured by Vivien the whole night. Of course, I never would've admitted this to her.

The truth was that Vivien and Shirin's boyfriends seemed to like them for *who they were.* The Dutch boy called Princess on the house phone every night to the delirious squeals of all the girls on the floor. Omar sent Vivien a rose daily via courier, turning every last Pierponter green with envy. It was as if the whole school had been stricken with the love disease or something. It was making me seriously cranky. Only listening to music helped. The Rolling Stones and Jimi Hendrix, in particular. If I ever outgrow Jimi Hendrix, I'll be ready to die.

By the time the following weekend rolled around, I'd pretty much had it. Fit to be tied, bored out of my mind, and smoking too much. I thought of going over to the equestrian center and taking one of the Arabians out for a ride but I was nervous about doing this without Shirin. (She was out on her riding date with the Dutch boy. This was a girl who'd looked up from her math books maybe twice the summer before, okay?) Sure, it was amazing that she'd brought over those stallions just for us. But between Vivien's broken elbow and the frenzy over their new boyfriends, I'd ridden my phenomenal quadruped once in two weeks. Talk about a waste.

After brunch, I decided to take off by myself. I needed to get away from Estrogen Central and treat myself to an adventure. I slipped a screwdriver into my back pocket—you never know when it might come in handy—and fled. Vivien spied me walking down the school's driveway and chased after me. She was the last person I wanted to see. After her steamy ice cream date with Omar, she couldn't talk about anything else. It was Omar this, and Omar that, until I was ready to push them both off a high cliff.

"Where are you going?" Vivien was breathless.

"Away from this place."

"Can I come?"

"If you have to ask, I don't think so."

"I wouldn't mind getting away for a while. You know, Shirin went off riding with—"

"I damn well know where she is, and where you were, and what you said, and what he did, and what she said, and—shit! I'm sick of hearing about it!"

"Fine, but where are you going?" Vivien was having a hard time keeping up with me. My legs were easily twice as long as hers. Plus her plaster-encased elbow, which moved like a clumsy piston, slowed her down considerably. At least her aggravating color disorder was subsiding.

"Destination unknown," I answered flatly.

"Sounds good to me," she said, sticking to me like a fly to shit.

As we walked through town, Vivien pointed out the ice cream shop where she and Omar had shared a chocolate sundae.

"I'd wanted extra nuts but he's allergic so—"

The look on my face made her stop in midsentence.

"Never mind."

The next thing we knew, we were on the edge of the high-way hitchhiking west. It didn't take long for us to get a ride. A middle-aged man with a caterpillar moustache asked us where we were going. Vivien and I looked at each other with blank expressions.

Then to my surprise, Vivien chirped: "Paris."

"Yeah, Paris," I echoed, warming to the prospect.

"I'm going as far as Geneva. Can I drop you there?"

"Sure," I said. "Sounds good."

The hour ride to Geneva was awkward and mostly silent. I half expected the guy to try to hit on us, or suggest a place for us to stay, something creepy like that. I'd done enough hitch-hiking in Canada to know what to expect but this was nothing like that. The guy, I swear to God, was a watchmaker who said he was going to Geneva to visit his mother. He figured we were from Pierpont and out for a joyride. He didn't chastise us, or threaten to report us.

All he said was this: "I wish I'd had the courage to live the life I'd wanted."

"What life was that?" Vivien asked. She never had a hard time talking to total strangers or asking personal questions.

"I wanted to go to Africa as a young man. To the diamond mines."

"My dad goes all the time," Vivien said sympathetically.

The man looked at each of us in turn, smiled enigmati-cally, and said nothing more.

Geneva turned out to be a colossal bore. I would've taken the boonies of Ontario over this fake, perfectly mani-cured city. Nobody stepped on the immaculate grass in the immaculate parks. The shops were as neat and gleaming as the synchronized clock towers. Nobody hurried or ran, as if they'd been born with built-in speed control mechanisms. I wanted thrift stores and outdoor cafés, motorcycles and mayhem, heroin addicts. Instead Vivien and I had to settle for raclette at a cutesy chalet restaurant with blue-aproned waitresses.

"Maybe we should've hitchhiked to Paris," I said glumly, pushing the boiled potatoes around on my plate. The clinging bits of parsley made me want to scream.

"Mmm, this is delicious," Vivien said, twirling a wad of melted cheese on her fork and shoving it in her mouth. "I'm glad things taste normal again. All that excess color was driving me crazy."

I tried not to imagine her lips entangled with Omar's. Instead I imagined the cheese congealing in Vivien's stomach, obstructing her digestion for weeks. I wanted to blame her for this nonstarter of an afternoon. On my own, things might've been different. I could've met an explorer going off to the Sahara. Or a wild girl to go cruising with on the Riviera, someone who'd think nothing of going topless. Maybe I would've shoplifted an emerald necklace just for the hell of it, and sold it at a pawn shop. Anything to counter this arid, bourgeois hell.

"Should we try and buy a couple of handguns?" I asked Vivien, trying to shake things up.

"Huh?"

"You know how to shoot them, don't you?"

"Yeah, but it's not the kind of thing you do casually. Maybe if your life was threatened."

"My life is threatened," I spat out.

"Oh?" Vivien was scraping the last of the raclette off her plate.

"By fucking boredom."

Vivien laughed and shrugged it off. Like ha, ha just another hilarious, over-the-top utterance by wacky Ingrid. She had no idea how desperate I felt, how close I was to unleashing the full brunt of my jealousy-fueled (there, I admitted it) wrath on her. But I managed, miraculously, to keep it together.

The most exciting part of the day happened when we returned. The headmistress and Vivien's father, newly arrived from the diamond mines of Africa, were waiting for us on the front steps of Pierpont. Their expressions were, dare I say, hardly welcoming.

VIVIEN

Ingrid couldn't have been in a worse mood if she tried. All I'd wanted was to spend some time with her and she acted like she was doing me this big favor. I knew she was jealous of Omar and me but for some reason, neither of us blurted out the obvious. If I accused Ingrid of being jealous, it would seem like I was gloating, or being insensitive. If she admitted to being jealous, she'd look selfish and small-minded. Lose-lose all around. So we kept our mouths shut.

Our walk back to Pierpont was tense, broken only by the sight of Papi and Madame Godenot in a near headlock at the entrance, presumably over our absence. Whatever it was, it didn't look good.

"Looks like some shit is about to hit the fan," Ingrid said with a smirk.

A part of me wanted to smack her. But the more sensible part of me knew I needed her fast-talking charm to get us out of this mess. Ingrid was a veteran of mess.

"What do we do now?" I whispered like a bad ventriloquist, trying not to move my lips.

"Just leave it to me, okay?" Ingrid looked straight at my father and the headmistress with a quasi-contrite smile.

"If I were you, Mademoiselle Baum, I wouldn't be so cheerful," Madame Godenot barked.

"Before you jump to conclusions, let me explain."

Oh, Ingrid was cool all right, unruffled. Nothing rattled her. I, on the other hand, was sweating buckets. All I managed to say was: "Uh . . . uh . . . uh. . . ."

"You"—the headmistress pointed at Ingrid—"go straight to your room. I will summon you at the appropriate time."

The second I heard "summon," I knew this wouldn't sit well with Ingrid. Nobody "summoned" Ingrid. Instead of proceeding to her room, Ingrid simply turned around and marched back down Pierpont's oak-lined driveway. No amount of glowering insistence on the part of the headmistress made her return. I thought she'd pop a vein in fury. Meanwhile, Ingrid kept growing smaller and smaller until she disappeared into the labyrinth of Rolle.

By the time Madame Godenot turned her attention to me, she looked like a psychotic beet. I glanced over at Papi, trying to get a read on him, but he looked more bemused than anything. He'd survived World War II, the Cuban revolution, bombs from murderous compatriots in Miami. What could an afternoon of teenage hijinks mean to him?

"Please, follow me, Vivien . . . and you, too, Max." The headmistress's voice softened.

Max? My father had barely arrived and they were already on a first-name basis? Madame Godenot led us to her office, sashaying more than walking. Something was up. Did they know each other from another life? Her guard dog secretary wasn't there on account of it being Sunday, and it felt eerily quiet, the kind of quiet that happens in horror films before the ax murderer bursts in.

"May I offer you some tea, Max?"

There it was again. Did I detect a note of flirtation? This couldn't be happening. It was too gruesome to contemplate.

"*Non merci, cherie.*"

My head swiveled so hard it could've snapped right off. "You speak French?"

"Enough to get by." Papi chuckled seductively, and Madame Godenot joined him.

"Can someone please tell me what's going on?"

"Should I tell her, Max?"

"Tell me what?"

"I'll do it, *cherie.*"

"Will you please stop calling her that, Dad? I mean, it's very weird, to say the least."

"Not under the circumstances, *mi amor.*"

Now he was purposely showing off his linguistic skills.

"You see, Vivien: Margot and I met in South Africa right after the war and—"

"Margot?! How do you know her first name? And when were you ever in South Africa? Jesus, Dad!"

"It was years before I met your mother."

"I was young and sailing in a race—"

"You two know each other. I mean *knew* each other?!"

"We were lovers for a short time and—"

"Oh my God!" I shouted, covering my ears. "I don't want to hear about it!"

"A long time ago"—my father raised his voice but I pretended not to hear him—"I was in love with Margot, but—"

"It was not our time," Madame Godenot finished his sentence.

"When Margot called me in the spring over this matter with your Iranian friend, I was surprised to discover that she was the same woman who I—"

"Let's say we're getting reacquainted."

"Yes, reacquainted."

Papi explained how the ship he'd taken in Nice had been forced to detour to South Africa. He was stranded in Johannesburg for two months before managing to talk his way onto another ship (he was totally broke by then) that set sail for Havana. In Johannesburg, he'd found a temporary job as a busboy in the city's most exclusive yacht club and one summer Sunday, beautiful like today, he'd met Margot.

I started to cry, harder and harder, until I was shaking, soggy, disheveled. It wasn't a matter of my father's youthful affair with my headmistress, or that she might become his girlfriend again, though this was gruesome enough. (Papi's other affair was more abstract somehow. At least that woman wasn't directly involved in my daily life.) What I was crying for was everything else, for what we'd lost and would never get back: Cuba, and the good times in Miami, my parents' marriage, my grandmother and Tía Cuca, and our lives, which would never be the same again.

SHIRIN

I had not been on a date before so I did not know what to expect. Back home, unmarried girls never went anywhere alone, much less with a boy, without imperiling their reputations. Teenagers were permitted to socialize, of course, but always under the watchful eyes of trusted chaperones. To be seen with a boy not your cousin or brother was to bring dishonor upon your family. So it was not without some degree of trepidation that I approached my afternoon rendezvous with Jan-Peter.

He and I met at Le Rosey's equestrian center, which was a good deal fancier than Pierpont's. The horses were in excellent shape, lively and with healthy coats, and the quality of the equipment was first-rate. They had a dining area adjacent to the rings, where you could comfortably watch the workouts and competitions. I arrived early, thinking it would be to my advantage, but Jan-Peter was already waiting for me. This made me unaccountably nervous. In broad daylight, without candles or music, would we find anything to say to each other? I froze to the spot. My kissing lesson with Ingrid flooded back to me and I blushed to the tips of my ears. Could I truly kiss this boy again?

"Shirin." Jan-Peter rushed up to me. "I was afraid you might change your mind."

He looked as pink as I felt, flushed and jittery, as if he could not believe I would show up.

"You look exactly the same," he joked.

I looked down at myself. I was wearing the identical outfit I had worn to the garden party. I needed a pithy response but no words would come. It felt as though someone had surgically closed off my throat.

Jan-Peter looked at me, expectant. His eyes were kind and curious. Soundlessly I went up to him, eyes wide open, and kissed him hard on the lips. I even dipped my tongue into his mouth, which startled him, and caused a ripple of tittering around the riding ring. When I pulled my face away, Jan-Peter looked dizzy and scared and pleased all at once.

"Is this how you say hello in your country?"

I stared back at him, still mute.

"Well, Shirin, I'm in favor of it." He laughed. "Would you like to get something to eat first? Or should we get straight to riding?"

I pointed toward the stables.

"So that would be horses first?"

I nodded curtly.

"I hope you don't mind my asking, Shirin, but is there some reason you're not talking? I mean, do you have laryngitis or something?"

With all the force I could muster, I concentrated on forming words but only managed to emit a few elongated diphthongs: ". . . aiaaiaaaee . . . eoeeeaea . . . oiooaoaooa . . ." What in heaven's name was happening to me? I tried to cover up my embarrassment by kissing him again. Jan-Peter looked dazed by my second attack. I longed to glue my face to his, if only to get my bearings. We were attracting a fair bit of attention.

Mercifully, Jan-Peter still had the presence of mind to take my hand and lead me to the stables. He had a pair of beautiful horses set up for us. Mine was all white and named, unimaginatively, Snow. His was all black and named, unimaginatively, Coal. Would Snow and Coal get along? Would Coal melt Snow? Would Snow freeze to ice and outrun Coal? Would these ridiculous questions stop crowding my normally high-functioning brain? I smiled idiotically at Jan-Peter and climbed onto the horse. Thank goodness for muscle memory.

After the embarrassing first fifteen minutes of my date with Jan-Peter, things fell into place. A few minutes of riding through the cooling woods loosened my tongue. Soon we were talking easily, chasing each other across meadows, fording streams, racing along the edge of a dairy farm (I won). Jan-Peter was a good rider; excellent, in fact. I would say I had very nearly met my match.

An hour or so later, we tied up our horses by a grove of poplars to let them rest (these were not Arabians, after all). Jan-Peter pulled a blanket from his satchel and invited me to sit down next to him. He had packed a modest picnic: French bread, a hunk of Dutch cheese, salami, a bottle of wine. Was he trying to seduce me? I told him that I'd thought we'd be having lunch at the equestrian club. But he only smiled and answered that he wanted to keep our options open.

"We can eat later again, if you wish," he joked.

That put me at ease. I had barely taken a sip of wine when he began kissing me with the same ardor I had kissed him. Our mouths fit together perfectly and I liked the taste of him, the smell of him, mingled with the sweat of the horses and the green breathing trees. I was grateful to Ingrid for teaching me the kissing basics and I put them to good use, licking his top lip and gently tugging on his lower one with my teeth. In between, we taught each other phrases in Farsi and Dutch. Jan-Peter had a superb ear and mimicked my every inflection. I taught him a series of curses that he repeated so convincingly that I actually blushed.

"Pedar sag!" he growled like an angry Iranian issuing the worst possible insult. It meant "Your father is a dog."

Jan-Peter shared with me a story about his family. He said that his great-grandmother, Taatje, who had lived to 102, had hidden a Jewish man in her basement for nearly a year during World War II. She had kept him alive, unbeknownst to the rest of the family, with boiled turnips and stale bread.

Then I told him something that nobody outside my family (except Vivien) knew: that my maternal grandmother was half Jewish and that she had suffered multiple mental breakdowns, in part due to her family's secret history. In the tumult of late-nineteenth-century pogroms, *her* father had escaped from Russia and crossed the border into Persia. He took a new name, Amir Ghaffari, and for decades hid his identity in order to survive. Only on his deathbed, did he confess the truth, and urged his family to move to Palestine. This past was of great concern to my father, who, as a member of the royal family, was supposed to be a sworn enemy of Israel.

The stories we exchanged made me feel closer to Jan-Peter.

"Now it is your turn to teach me Dutch," I insisted, changing the subject. "Something off-color." I was surprised at my audacity.

Jan-Peter offered to teach me the language of Amsterdam's red light district. (Had he been there?) But after his first phrase—"Using the back door will cost you double"—I withdrew my request.

After that, we grew quiet for awhile and lay down, looking up through the canopies of leaves. Squirrels scampered along the limbs and a blue jay screeched its complaint to the heavens. Tentatively, Jan-Peter reached over and touched my left breast. It seemed to arch under his touch, tingling, like when I walked out of the sea into chilly air.

"Is that okay?" he asked, resting his hand there.

"I think so."

Soon Jan-Peter's hand drifted down my belly before flattening his palm between my legs. He started rubbing me there, through my riding pants, gently circling with his middle finger. I was afraid that he would try to force himself inside me like that boor from last year's garden party. But Jan-Peter only kept circling as my pleasure increased. For a moment, I imagined my whole family looking down at me from the tops of the poplars. What would they think to see me here alone with this boy? This boy with his hand between their precious Shirin's legs? Would they call me a whore?

"I'm not sure about this," I said, stopping his hand with mine. The good feeling lingered. Then Jan-Peter nestled his head against my shoulder and began kissing my neck. Goose bumps radiated down my arms and legs. What was happening to me? I finished my wine and suggested that we continue riding. I liked being with him but I was growing anxious.

As I was adjusting my saddle, Jan-Peter took off, shouting: "Catch me if you can!"

I spurred my horse and chased after him, galloping hard. The tingling between my legs grew more intense the faster

I rode but I kept pushing to catch up with him. When the nose of my horse was parallel to the tail of his, I felt it. A sweet explosion that coursed up and down my body and left me, momentarily, weak. Abruptly, I stopped my horse. My face was hot and my nipples tightened and pushed against my blouse.

Jan-Peter turned his horse around and trotted over to see what was wrong. I was sweating under my helmet and my back felt damp. I held the reins high to hide my breasts.

"You look very pink," he said. "How do you say that in Farsi?"

I told him and he said it so perfectly that I had to laugh.

DAY
EIGHTEEN

INGRID

With Vivien and Shirin preoccupied with their respective boyfriends, my presence wasn't exactly needed around Pierpont.
So after that tense encounter with the headmistress and company, I went AWOL for three days. It was amazing how easily
you could get around with a credit card and a reasonably intact
appearance. I knew that Madame Godenot would be going ber-
serk over my disappearance and call my parents. But they'd
been through this before. My mother would check with the
credit card company, find out that I was charging up meals and
hotels—in short, that I was *alive*—and basically give it a rest.
This past year, something had snapped with them. It wasn't
like they'd stopped caring, but they had essentially given up on
me. It'd become an ingrained law of Baum family physics that
the more you tried to control Ingrid, the more out of control

Ingrid became. Their new approach was simple: to let me do whatever the hell I pleased.

I wish I could report that I'd done something daring and inimitable during my escape from Pierpont, that I'd learned to fly helicopters or saved triplet orphans from a burning building. Nothing all that exciting actually happened. I hopped on a train to Munich and spent two and a half days walking around the city, which was in high gear getting ready for the summer Olympics in August. There was no real rhyme or reason to where I went or what I did.

In the Englischer Garten, I stumbled across a nudist section and got a pretty varied (that is to say, nasty) cross-section of humanity there. There were grandmothers with flopping breasts and hirsute, concave-chested guys communing with trees. My favorite was a bunch of naked teenagers playing table tennis. When they invited me to join them, I didn't know if it was for the table tennis or the nudity. I demurred. Maybe I wasn't as free with my body as I'd thought.

Most of all, I was trying to imagine what the city had been like when my father was growing up there, when Hitler's rise seemed so inevitable that Vati joined the Nazi cause. He never talked about those days. My impression was that he spent a good portion of his energy trying to repress the past. That first afternoon in Munich, I went to the Nymphenburg Palace, a baroque monstrosity, and dropped in at the Alte Pinakothek to look at the Rubens paintings. It made my own drawings seem pathetically inadequate.

My second day there, I walked into an exhibit on Der Blaue Reiter group of expressionist artists, who'd worked in Munich at the turn of the century. Imagine Paul Klee,

Wassily Kandinsky, Alexej von Jawlensky, and Gabriele Münter all hanging out together in 1911. Their paintings were amazing, saturated with color and disturbing dreams. Damn, I was sixty years too late for that party.

That night, I got shitfaced at the Hofbrau House (nobody asked for your ID in Germany) and I had to fight off a group of idiot American businessmen who were outbidding each other for my company. "Three hundred dollars!" a bleary-eyed Texan shouted before I got up and left, flipping them off on my way out. It made me wonder whether normal relations were even possible between men and women. It seemed to me that you had to be either nine years old or on death's door to have an intelligent conversation with a member of the opposite sex.

Was it me? Maybe I gave off a "Come fuck me" vibe or something. Whatever, it was pretty depressing.

I walked and walked until my legs got sore, mostly people-watching and fantasizing about their lives. I kept framing them in my mind, trying to freeze them forever at the particular moment in time that I'd noticed them. I wondered what they were thinking about, who they were in love with, what secrets they kept. Would they ever guess that a stranger had scrutinized them so closely?

There was a cute guy—bearded, intense-looking, perfect lips—tending a coffee bar near the university. After four heavily-sugared espressos, I was so wired I could've flapped my wings and flown on my own power. Still, he didn't make a move. He was probably a philosophy major. Those guys were all talk and no action. In any case, I was tired of always being the one to make the overtures. Hadn't Shirin and Vivien's

boyfriends—I still couldn't believe they even had boyfriends—
come after *them*? And nicely, too. Why did I have to get the
drunken tourists?

I felt lonely in Munich, and out of place.

On the long train ride back to Switzerland, I kept thinking
about those Rubens paintings. It's not that I was particularly
interested in the subject matter—how many fat, pink-thighed
cherubs can you paint in a lifetime, for Christ's sake?—but
there was no denying Rubens's brilliance, his exquisite eye.
What was there left to do in painting after him? After the
Impressionists? Der Blaue Reiter? After the abstract expres-
sionists? After the minimalists and pop artists?

Then I got to thinking about photography, how it was
in its relative infancy as an art form. A lot of people didn't
even believe photography was art, merely technology. Aim,
shoot, develop. There was your picture. But I'd seen enough
good photography at exhibits in Toronto to know they were
wrong. The more I thought about it, the more agitated I
became. By the time we pulled into Geneva, I practically
leaped off the train and ran through the nearby streets hunting for a photo shop. I barged in to the first one I saw and
picked out a really nice camera. I charged it to my father's
credit card along with thirty rolls of black-and-white film, a
tripod, and a camera bag.

When I returned to Pierpont late Wednesday afternoon
carrying my equipment, nothing had changed. It was the
same bucolic bubble of a place that I'd left seventy-two hours
earlier. Nobody there thought about anything significant.
Nobody cared about the world beyond these gates. I wanted
to capture the indifferent beauty and insularity of the place

and broadcast it to the world. A PHOTOGRAPHIC ESSAY ON PRIVILEGE, FROM THE INSIDE . . . by Ingrid Baum. I imagined it appearing in *Life* magazine, or *National Geographic*, right next to the topless African women harvesting yams. If you thought about it, Pierpont was no less exotic.

Before I was halfway up the driveway, I got another idea for a photo shoot. I turned around and headed straight for the taxi stand in Rolle.

"To the Pierpont equestrian center," I ordered the driver.

As we headed into the countryside, the warm, late-afternoon light suffused everything it touched. I loaded my camera and trekked over to the riding ring. Lessons were underway. The harsh, high voice of one of the equestrian teachers rang out over the thudding of hooves in the dirt. Madame Gert sounded like a cross between an eagle and a sea lion. And with her beaked nose and pronounced facial hair, she looked like an unhappy product of the two.

I went to the far end of the stables where Shirin kept her Arabian stallions. All three—Asad, Bahman, and Cyrus— were there, alert and magnificent. I opened their gates one at a time and they blinked at me with what I imagined to be a grateful conspiracy.

"Follow me," I said. To my amazement, they did.

I led them to a back pasture and they came along quietly, curious as to what I would do. I picked up my camera and started shooting the horses from every angle. At first they didn't move, hypnotized by me and my camera. Maybe they were listening to the whirring sound of advancing film. I kept changing the aperture, focusing sharp, then soft. I didn't really know what I was doing but I was flushed with excitement. I snapped through that first roll very quickly and fumbled to load my second one.

The Arabians waited patiently until I shot two more rolls of film.

"Thanks, guys," I whispered and they seemed to understand. Then, half joking, I shouted: "Action!"

Do you know what they did then? Bahman, Asad, and Cyrus started galloping in an endless circle. For me. For my pictures. In the day's last light. They looked suspended in air, gliding effortlessly through space, stopping time. It was supernaturally beautiful. Miraculously, I captured it. Call it beginner's luck. Call it divine intervention. Call it whatever you want. But it seemed to me that those horses knew what they were doing. It wouldn't be an exaggeration to say that Shirin's Arabian stallions saved my life.

DAY
TWENTY-ONE

VIVIEN

It wasn't enough that my father had left my mother in New York over some buxom floozy fifteen years his junior. That previous winter in New York, it seemed that all of my friends' fathers were leaving their wives for their secretaries, or nurses, or Pan Am stewardesses. Midlife crises were contagious, like the influenza pandemic that wiped out fifty million people in 1918. Papi's betrayal was horrible in itself. But nothing prepared me, nothing could've prepared me, for the seismic disaster of my father falling in love (again, he tried to assure me) with my headmistress.

Madame Godenot was educated, and reasonably attractive, and close to Papi's age. One could argue that she was a definite step up from the floozy. But she was not my mother. It was hideously embarrassing to have my own father hanging around my boarding school most of the summer, mooning over the headmistress. I was the one who was supposed to be having a romance here. But as usual, everything had to revolve around him.

Dad wanted me to go out to dinner with the two of them to discuss my "problem," but I wouldn't hear of it. Go out with him and Madame Godenot like we were some cozy trinity of a family? No way I could do this.

As a kid, I never got into fights with my father, much less the screaming matches that were becoming our norm. I'd often defended Papi against my mother's charges. When she called him a lunatic for confronting the Cuban exile community, I called him brave. When she accused him of being a workaholic, I shot back that he was working for us. When Mami freaked out that he was carrying a gun, I surreptitiously joined him at the shooting range. Solidarity was our modus operandi. In fact, I was a lot more like my father than my mother. This made the current situation even more painful.

Why had I bothered sticking up for him all those years when he didn't think twice about betraying me?

Although I refused to dine with Papi and the headmistress, I did relent to go with just him. He said to choose any restaurant I wanted, so I decided to stick it to him at Chez Henri, where entrées cost something like forty dollars. If he was taking me out for an apology dinner, I wanted to make him pay big-time. For what he did to Mami. For what he was doing to me.

Before the dinner, I consulted with my roommates over what strategy to take.

"Castrate him." This was Ingrid's suggestion. "It's the only way to stop a pervert."

"You only think he is a pervert because he is somebody's father," Shirin retorted.

"He's not just somebody's father, Shirin. He's *my* father."

"And a pervert," Ingrid added for good measure.

"Look, he is just a man. And he is in love—"

"Ugh! Don't say that!" I cried.

"At least he isn't gay." Ingrid chuckled. "Imagine the buzz around here if the headmistress were a headmaster. Whoa."

"Oh, that's helpful. Thanks very much." I was on the verge of tears. How was I going to make it through an entire dinner? I was going to eat at one of the finest restaurants in Europe, something I'd ordinarily be ecstatic about, and my stomach felt like a vat of acid.

"Look, Vivi-*joon*, life takes many turns. You cannot control your father, or the decisions he makes in his life. Trying to twist them toward your will is futile, like struggling against a wind that will soon pass."

"Since when did you start channeling the Buddha?" Ingrid sneered.

"I am quite serious, my sweet. Allow your father to speak. Listen to him. Do not judge him. You are his daughter, no matter what happens. It is better to give blessings than rain curses on another's head."

"Where the hell does she come up with this stuff?" Ingrid picked up her camera and was focusing on a close-up of Shirin and me. Ever since her purportedly life-changing trip to Munich, Ingrid had become a shutterbug. You couldn't sneeze without her taking an action shot. "Move closer together, will you? Look engaged."

"We were engaged until you interrupted us," Shirin bristled.

"Look this way. Keep the intensity," Ingrid instructed us. "I still say the man should be locked away with child molesters. A little buggering might do him a world of good."

"This is my father we're talking about. Not one of your dim-witted farm boys." I was furious with her. How dare she talk about Papi like that?

"Oh, I see," Ingrid said, lowering her camera. "So that's what you think of me? Only capable of dating a bunch of sheep fuckers? Well, not all of us can get inexplicably lucky and land a big fish like Tunisian poster boy."

"Inexplicably?"

"It is evident that Ingrid cannot abide our happiness." Shirin said this as if it were a law of physics.

"So this is what it's all about?" I spat out the words. "Boys?"

Ingrid lifted her camera again and started shooting. If she'd had a gun in her hands, she couldn't have been more aggressive.

I held both arms out in front of me, covering my face.

"I thought you were the one who said that you had no respect for girls who let boys get in the way of their friendships."

"Yes, this is correct," Shirin interjected. "She did say that."

"I thought *you* were the adventurous, cynical, sisterhood-is-everything feminist here. Uses boys and discards them. Doesn't believe in love. Pretends to give everyone strictly utilitarian advice."

Ingrid continued shooting, ignoring my tirade.

We were interrupted by a knock on the door. It was my

father with *her* at his side. He was beaming, oblivious to my distress. Madame Godenot was wearing a beaded ivory silk number that could've doubled as an elegant, second-marriage wedding dress. What, was she rehearsing already?

"I thought you said we were going to dinner alone," I mumbled.

"We are, *mi amor*, but Margot wanted to see us off."

"Well, now that you've seen them, be off!" That was Ingrid coming to my rescue. She looked angry enough to throw a wrench at the headmistress. Instead she kept taking pictures. I loved Ingrid as fiercely as I detested her at that moment.

"That will be enough from you, Mademoiselle Baum," Madame Godenot snapped. "You're already walking a very fine line with me this summer."

Ingrid took Madame Godenot's picture in response. I couldn't wait to see what this latest batch of photographs would look like.

"Well, good night, girls," my father said magnanimously. "Should we bring you back some dessert?"

"Sure, a hot-fudge sundae." Ingrid rolled her eyes, then resumed clicking away.

"*Bon appétit,*" Shirin called out after us as we retreated down the hallway.

Needless to say, dinner was an absolute nightmare. Except for the food, of course. It was all I could do not to pelt Papi with his own snails in butter sauce. I was almost too upset to eat. (I said *almost.*) What I remember best was a succulent rack of lamb and an *île flottant à la pistache* for dessert. Everything else was a blur. As for my father, he refused to be dissuaded from his latest folly.

DAY
TWENTY-SIX

SHIRIN

I did not know for days that what I had experienced was an orgasm. I had ridden horses for many years and such a thing had never happened to me. Of course, I had not gone riding alone before with a boy to whom I found myself attracted.

The way I learned that what I had experienced was an orgasm occurred entirely by accident. In the bathtub a few days later (our suite had the only bathtub on our floor), I was thinking about my date with Jan-Peter when the tingling between my legs resurged. I reached down and rubbed myself, like he had done, circling and circling with my finger until the explosive feeling came over me again. I repeated this until I was exhausted with pleasure.

I might have drowned in that bathtub if Ingrid had not

pounded on the door, needing to use the toilet. When I emerged, she took one look at me and said: "Ah, so I see our princess has discovered orgasms. Well, it's about goddamn time."

DAY
TWENTY-SEVEN

VIVIEN

It was nearly the end of summer and I'd hardly seen Omar at all. My heart wasn't in the relationship anymore, distracted as I was with my father's affair. Papi started referring to Madame Godenot as the *lost love* of his life, and had practically moved onto campus. It was disgusting. If she was the lost love of his life, what did that make me? The wretched offspring of a marriage of convenience?

Everyone at Pierpont knew about their fling (I refused to call it anything but that) and teased me mercilessly. You wouldn't believe the nicknames people came up with for my father and the headmistress. Let's just say "geriatric love birds" was one of the kinder ones. It was beyond embarrassing. Every night, Madame Godenot could be seen leaving Pierpont in increasingly sexy outfits (miniskirts were back in style) to meet my father at the Hotel Belmont, which Ingrid rechristened the Love Shack.

Even the boys at Le Rosey had heard about the affair. The last time I saw Omar, he asked me as delicately as he could: "Is your father, eh, having relations with your head-mistress?" At least he didn't use one of the coarser terms in circulation, like *hammering* or *stuffing*. It couldn't get any more humiliating.

When I told him it was true, he looked at me sympatheti-cally. That was probably the worst thing he could've done. I didn't want his sympathy. And I definitely didn't want his pity. I decided to stop seeing him. I didn't want to be in love with anyone. If everything ended badly anyway, I'd rather spare myself the heartache. When Omar called in the eve-nings, I refused to come to the hall phone. I returned the flowers he sent me. He wrote me poetry, which I might've liked if I hadn't been determined to ignore him.

Strangely enough, the more I rejected him, the more interested he became.

"It's all about the hunt," Ingrid pronounced when I com-plained that I couldn't get rid of him.

It was a touchy subject because Ingrid had liked Omar ever since that first party at Le Rosey. But, luckily, she was now possessed by photography, and nothing else seemed to matter. She'd started begging Shirin and me to pose nude for her. For art's sake, she insisted. To my utter shock, Shirin was actually considering the proposal. Had everyone gone stark raving mad?

It probably shouldn't have come as a surprise to me then when Omar climbed in our bedroom window on our second-to-last night of camp. Around three in the morning, he came crashing in, bleeding and studded with thorns from the rose trellis. Ingrid shone her industrial strength flashlight on him and shouted "Halt!" just like in World War II movies.

"Rise and shine, ladies! We have a visitor!" Ingrid had Omar on the ground with his hands tied behind his back, and a booted foot on the back of his head. (Did she actually sleep with her boots on?)

Omar looked like he was about to cry. His eyes pooled with tears and his whole face glistened in the sharp glare of Ingrid's flashlight.

"What the hell are you doing here?" I demanded.

"I . . . I . . ." He couldn't get the words out. The poor guy looked abjectly miserable trussed up on the floor.

For a moment, I noted how handsome he was but my fury dispelled any fleeting appreciation for his beauty. It was not, however, lost on Ingrid. Even with her boot on his head, I could see she was checking him out from behind. She couldn't help it. Ingrid lived beyond the confines of ordinary morality. I decided right then that she was, fundamentally, amoral. Maybe I didn't want Omar—at least not until I sorted out the mess with my father—but I certainly didn't want Ingrid honing in on the one boy who'd ever paid any attention to me.

Shirin came over to inspect the intruder, wrapping her embroidered silk robe around her. She looked glassy-eyed, like the time I'd hypnotized her. Without warning, she got down on all fours and brought her face about six inches from Omar's. He looked perturbed and not a little anxious. Maybe he thought she was going to torture him.

"Are you in love?" Shirin whispered softly.

"Is the pope Catholic?" Ingrid snapped.

Omar cracked his neck trying to nod. He seemed grateful for the opportunity to establish his amorous intentions.

"I told you this wasn't a good time, Omar!" I cried. "My life's falling apart. I don't have time to fall in love. I don't know what else I can say or do to make you go away." I slumped down on my bed and covered my face with my hands.

"You heard the lady," Ingrid barked. "Now scram!" She removed her boot from Omar's head and he swiveled it around, checking to see if it still worked.

"Wait," Shirin insisted. "I think we should give him an opportunity to speak. This young man is in love. He must be allowed to sing."

"Sing?!" Ingrid and I were incredulous.

"Yes, sing," Shirin said. "Every utterance of love is a song."

"Another installment of Mysticism for the Ages." Ingrid crossed her arms. "She'll have us whirling around like dervishes in no time."

"I . . . I . . . would like to s-s-sing," Omar said, visibly shaken from Ingrid's attack. Then he pulled a crumpled sheet of paper from his back pocket.

Ingrid decided this was too good a photographic opportunity to miss and set up her tripod. "Would you mind taking off your shirt?"

"No way." I grabbed her arm. "You can't do this."

"Why not?"

"I do not think it is appropriate to ask our guest to disrobe," Shirin interjected.

"Guest? The guy comes crashing in here in the middle of

the night. We could seriously bust him. Instead, I'm offering to take a few tasteful—"

"Uh, I don't think—" I reached for Ingrid's camera but she pulled it away.

"—*artistic* photographs of a young man in his prime and—"

"Prime, my ass!" I shrieked.

In the heat of battle, neither of us noticed that Omar was unbuttoning his shirt. When we looked over at him, he was naked from the waist up. Now there was really no denying his beauty. Even Shirin was mesmerized by Omar's perfect, muscled, lightly hairy chest. There was a distinct possibility that we might rush him and run our hands all over his perfect body.

"I don't mind posing for a few photographs," Omar said modestly. "But please allow me to say what I've come to say."

The three of us were slack-jawed and staring at him. Omar held up the sheet of paper he'd retrieved from a back pocket and cleared his throat. Before he began to read, he prefaced it with a few words of his own: "I am forlorn that my poetry has not moved you sufficiently, my dear Vivien. It is for this reason that I have turned to a maestro for assistance. Please beg my indulgence as I borrow his words to say what is in my heart."

Even Ingrid stopped taking pictures long enough to listen

So that you will hear me
my words
sometimes grow thin
as the tracks of the gulls on the beaches . . .

Before you they peopled the solitude that you occupy,
and they are more used to my sadness than you are.

Now I want them to say what I want to say to you
to make you hear as I want you to hear me.

The wind of anguish still hauls on them as usual.
Sometimes hurricanes of dreams still knock them over.
You listen to other voices in my painful voice.

Lament of old mouths, blood of old supplications.
Love me, companion. Don't forsake me. Follow me.
Follow me, companion, on this wave of anguish.

But my words become stained with your love.
You occupy everything, you occupy everything.

I am making them into an endless necklace
for your white hands, smooth as grapes.

After Omar finished, nobody said a word for the longest time. Then quietly, without insistence, Omar put on his shirt, slowly buttoned it, and climbed out the window the way he came. We could hear his footsteps on the gravel, then complete silence as he made his way across the damp grass and away from Pierpont, perhaps forever. I wasn't sure what I felt at that moment. I didn't know whether I would change my mind about Omar. I didn't know if I could persuade my father to come to his senses and return home. I didn't know whether I would ever be capable of falling in love. All I knew was that the poem Omar had read to us—to me—was sacred. And nothing, nothing could desecrate it.

DAY TWENTY-EIGHT

INGRID

On the last morning of our second summer at Pierpont, I got Vivien and Shirin to pose for me nude. Maybe it was the incredible magic of the night before, which seemed, to borrow a phrase, like a midsummer night's dream. Maybe it was that we'd already been through so much together that all that remained was trust. Maybe it was that trust that enabled me to take such stunning photographs of my cherished friends. Before I had to beg either of them again, my roommates were nude, unself-consciously so, and posing for me. What I saw through my lens were not my dear friends but the stunning topographies of two bodies on the cusp of womanhood—landscapes of skin and innocence. Vivien and Shirin were beautiful to me in their nakedness, and their trust. They *presented* themselves to me with sweet frankness. And this, more than anything, I'm convinced, was what ultimately shone through.

CODA

December 7, 1972

Dear Vivien and Shirin,

I've copied this letter to both of you because I don't have the patience to write this twice. Huge news! I've gotten my first gallery show. It's going to open in Toronto on March 9 and you must come. No excuses. I'm supposed to get releases from each of you saying that you agree to let me show nude photographs of you since we're underage (what a joke, right?). Forms attached. I know you'll say YES and then dance naked with me at the opening. More details to come. Please write and let me know what's happening in Tehran and NYC.

Love and solidarity,

Ingrid

✳

10 January 1973

Dearest Vivien,

*Just a quick note from Gstaad where my family is skiing.
This postcard is of the chalet we've rented. I wish you
were here but I know you'd probably spend the whole
time reading by the fireplace or baking strudel. I miss you
and send you a snowball!*

Love,

Shirin

❋

Excerpt from the *Toronto Sun*, FEBRUARY 23, 1973:
A controversy is raging in the art world over a
seventeen-year-old girl's prospective exhibit at a
Toronto gallery. Word has leaked that the photographs
by Ingrid Baum, a young artist from Wiarton, Ontario,
are pornographic in nature. Deus Ex Machina Gallery
is standing by its decision to display the photographs of
naked adolescents, as well as erotically charged images
of Arabian stallions.

"Art and decency don't even belong in the same sentence," says gallery owner Seth Bentley. "We're showing
these photographs because they are, most decidedly,
art. And there is no circumscribed age for art."

The newly formed antipornography group, Citizens Against Obscenity, is battling to prevent the show's opening. Countering their efforts is an international artists' petition strongly favoring Ms. Baum's right to show her work. Among the famous signatories of the six-hundred-strong petition: Andy Warhol, Robert Rauschenberg, and Polish filmmaker Roman Polanski.Reached at her Wiarton home, Ingrid Baum defended her right to exhibit the photographs and gave her interpretation of the scandal: "When a teenager co-opts the symbols of eroticism for herself, all hell breaks loose."

MARCH 9 1973 STOP CONGRATULATIONS ON YOUR OPENING STOP SING INGRID SING STOP I AM PROUD OF YOU STOP LOVE FROM YOUR FRIEND SHIRIN STOP PS PLEASE FORGIVE MY ABSENCE STOP I HAVE NOT BEEN WELL

March 10, 1973

Dearest Shirin,

I wish you could've been at Ingrid's opening tonight. It was the most amazing time ever. Ingrid wore head-to-toe leather and waved around a cigarette holder, every inch the artiste. People went nuts over her pictures and called her a genius. To add to the drama, a bunch of protesters

*outside carried nasty signs saying stuff like: FIGHT
CORRUPTION OF MINORS and OBSCENITY IS NOT
ART. News reporters were everywhere.*

*Anyway, both of us were smiling down on the crowd from
the walls of the gallery (Ingrid blew up our photographs
to larger-than-life size). It was embarrassing at first but
I weirdly got used to it. My Tía Cuca flew up with me to
Toronto and I noticed her lingering over one of the post-
midnight shots of—you guessed it—our very own bare-
chested Omar. Feisty woman, my aunt.*

*I can't believe it's four in the morning already. I'll write more
soon but just wanted to give you a hot-off-the-press report.*

Hugs and kisses,

Vivien

P.S. WE MISSED YOU, PRINCESS!!!! XO, INGRID

April 17, 1973

Dear Ingrid and Shirin,

*All points bulletin!!! My father is engaged to Madame
Godenot and they're planning a September wedding!
M.G. resigned from Pierpont and landed a teaching job*

*at the Alliance Française here in New York. I see her and
my father as little as humanly possible. Far from being
devastated, my mother has completely transformed
herself. She's lost thirty pounds, taken up cross-country
skiing, and gotten some kind of face treatment that makes
her look ten years younger. I hardly recognize her. To
make matters worse, she's started dating the divorced
investment banker father of a girl who goes to my school.
No one has boundaries anymore.*

*The only things keeping me sane are reading (I'm making
my way through the best Latin American authors in
translation) and my Saturday cooking classes at the
Culinary Institute of America. School is an endurance
test and I can't tell you what I'm studying except for
geometry, which I enjoy for some inexplicable reason.
Maybe it's the proofs, which are kind of like recipes.
They're the only things that make sense to me.*

*I'm assuming we're still on for Switzerland this summer.
I'm clinging to the idea of us together again as my life raft.
When all is said and done, nobody understands me better
than you two. Please forgive this disjointed letter. I miss
you both terribly.*

XOXO,

Vivien

BOOK THREE:

WHAT THE HEART WANTS

SUMMER 1973

DAY
ONE

VIVIEN

I stayed up most of the night on the flight to Geneva reading *One Hundred Years of Solitude.* I felt too old to be going away to summer camp at sixteen and would've never done it had it not been for Ingrid and Shirin. We thought of meeting up somewhere else but, in the end, we decided on Pierpont. It was the one familiar place in the world that we could live together for a summer with minimal interference. We could simply hang out and be friends.

It was difficult—not to mention exorbitant—to stay in touch with one another long-distance during the year. Letters took forever, especially from Iran; a month was the norm, even if the letters managed to make it the seven thousand miles. By then, whatever crisis we'd been having would long be over. A part of me kept thinking about Omar. Had I completely blown it with him? Maybe he was the love of my life and I hadn't realized it. I doubted that he'd bother returning to Le Rosey for another summer. Even if he did, why would he still be interested in me?

The amazing poem that Omar had read to us that night in our dorm room got me interested in Latin American literature in a big way. I mean, the guy was from Tunisia and reading poetry in translation from Chile. Not exactly your run-of-the-mill teenager. In retrospect, I was an idiot, plain and simple. Not a single boy in New York had so much as looked at me in the intervening months, much less mooned over me or written me poetry. On the plane to Switzerland, I prayed I'd get another chance.

After the usual arrival hassles, I got to Pierpont on one of the early busses. I traipsed up to the third floor to see if Ingrid or Shirin had arrived yet. No luck. That summer we had single rooms but made sure ahead of time that they'd be adjoining. I'd baked up a storm—fresh lime crisps and pistachio blondies—and packed them in tins for my friends. I signed up for Advanced French, Intensive Cooking, Beginning Horseback Riding (hope sprang eternal), and Introduction to Italian (a new afternoon option for the less athletically inclined).

I was surprised when Babette, our housekeeper—we had one to ourselves on the third floor—knocked on my door and handed me a note, requesting that I go to the headmistress's office *tout de suite*. My first instinct was to panic. Had something happened to my grandmother or Tía Cuca? I mean, it was impossible to be in trouble already. Ingrid hadn't even arrived yet. Maybe I was traumatized by headmistresses in general after my father decided to marry my old one.

The new headmistress, Madame Sarazin, was wrinkled but simply and elegantly dressed. She introduced herself as the former chemistry teacher at Pierpont, brought out of retirement to oversee the orderly transition from Madame Godenot's reign to the as-yet-undetermined new one. I figured we'd be able to run rings around her.

"Please sit down, Mademoiselle Wahl," she began, her rheumy blue eyes watching me carefully. "It's a pleasure to meet such a talented young woman."

"Talented?"

"The news of your culinary feats has spread far beyond our community."

"Really?" I was embarrassed and pleased at the same time.

"I'm quite delighted that you decided to return to Pierpont under the, eh, circumstances."

"Yeah, well, me too."

"I've called you to my office today with a proposal. There's to be an international culinary competition in Lausanne later this month. I was hoping that you might consider representing Pierpont at this event."

"What?" I blurted, barely containing myself.

"It's for promising young chefs whose names must be put forward by a sponsoring institution. The winner of the competition—and it is quite a strenuous one, I assure you, taking place over the course of a weekend—will be given a full scholarship to Le Cordon Bleu cooking school in Paris. The contest will be televised—"

"Oh my God!"

"And you will likely make many useful contacts. May I assume that this *concours* would interest you?"

"Yes!" I nearly jumped out of my seat. "I mean, I'd be very honored."

"I remember loving chemistry with a similar passion at your age," Madame Sarazin said, smiling. Her teeth were too perfect-looking to be real. "In fact, cooking is a branch of chemistry. A more pleasant-smelling one, *n'est-ce pas?* Although I would not advise ingesting . . ."

I didn't hear much more of her ramblings. I wondered if Chef d'Aubigné, or one of last year's instructors, had recommended me. A torrent of recipes filled my brain—seafood enchiladas, crab-stuffed salmon, vegetable *biryani*, homemade pesto. Would I have to cook an eight-course meal, or specialize in something particular, like dessert? I started salivating from nervousness or hunger, I wasn't sure which. I saw myself on television in a white uniform with a toque and fancy peppercorn grinder and . . . drooling. For God's sake, I was drooling.

INGRID

I didn't get to Pierpont until late that first night. By then, Vivien and Shirin were practically planning my funeral. There was no shortage of melodrama where the three of us were concerned. As I pulled up in an eggplant-colored Porsche convertible with a hot guy almost twenty years my senior (Gerhardt was thirty-six), the gossip alarm sounded. Soon everyone was hanging from the window shutters, bug-eyed, watching me disembark. When I gave my nouveau art-dealer boyfriend a slow, full-mouth kiss, the collective gasp was audible. Let's just say I've long known the value of a good entrance.

As Gerhardt zoomed off down the driveway, the gasping erupted into deafening chatter, as if every sparrow within a hundred miles had decided to roost in the eaves of Pierpont's dormitory. In the midst of the noise, I spotted Vivien and Shirin running toward me, megagrins on their faces.

Vivien looked pretty much the same, but I hardly recognized Shirin. She was heart-stoppingly gorgeous. I could've never imagined using this word to describe anyone my age: *womanly*. But that's what she'd become, a woman.

"Ingrid!" the two of them screamed, locking me in a sandwich embrace that knocked the wind out of me. Vivien started to cry, making her mascara run down her cheeks.

"Hey, let's get inside before they throw me out again." I laughed.

We made our way up past the first and second floors, site of our many adventures, and clambered to the third with my luggage in tow. A gaggle of younger girls followed us, barely keeping a discreet distance and whispering incessantly. *Famous*, I heard, and *bitch*, which probably summed me up as well as anything else I'd been called.

The three of us crowded into my room and unceremoniously slammed the door on the stragglers. There was way too much catching up to do to even think of sleeping.

"Okay, let's not beat around the bush," I began, sitting on my cushy bed *mit* down comforter. (The amenities really improved once you ascended to the third floor.) "Who got laid this year?"

"Uh, maybe we should start with you," Vivien insisted. "Was that guy down there Exhibit A, or what?"

"Yes, please inform us of your carnal activities," Shirin

said in a police inquisitor voice, which made us crack up.

"What do you want to know?" I teased.

"Everything," Vivien said. "Wait. Don't start yet. I've got treats." She ran to her room and brought over a tin of cookies.

"These are amazing." My mouth was full and crumbs tumbled everywhere. Then I pulled out a bottle of wine from one of my suitcases.

"Milk would go a lot better with my lime crisps." Vivien wrinkled her nose. But she accepted a plastic cup of my cabernet.

"To our reunion and to the carnal life." I held my cup up high for a toast then finished my drink in one gulp. My roommates followed suit. "So where were we?"

"Age? Rank? Serial number?" Shirin persisted.

"Ah, where to begin?" I feigned my best world-weary voice. It didn't take me long to tell the story, or at least the beginning of the story. I'd already spent three whole days and nights with Gerhardt in Zürich, preparing for my first solo photo exhibit in Europe. I knew that what I'd been experiencing with him was something far beyond the capacities of Ontario farm boys. Making love with Gerhardt was a gourmet experience—something Vivien would appreciate.

We spent hours in bed. We took baths together. We rubbed scented lotions all over each other. We fed each other fruit and cheese, stark naked. The man, I swear, could spend an hour lingering in the hollow of my neck or licking my left nipple. He made me come, and come again, in a way I'd only been able to do by myself. Scratch that—much better than I could do by myself. The guy was a one-man toolbox. Up until then, boys didn't seem to know what to do with my body except use it for their own selfish pleasures. Gerhardt was a revelation.

Vivien and Shirin listened to me, barely saying a word, murmuring now and then for emphasis and solidarity.

"Are you in love?" Vivien asked. "I know it's not your style but this sounds pretty serious."

"You cannot confuse love with lust, Vivi. They are two different creatures, like the tiger and the butterfly."

"Since when did you become the expert?" I ribbed, pouring myself another cup of wine. I knew I'd have a hangover the next day but I didn't care. Conjugating French verbs didn't require a full set of brain cells.

"As a matter of fact, I have my own news to report."

"Oh?"

"I, too, have been with a boy," Shirin said modestly.

"You what?" Vivien was incredulous.

"Define 'been,'" I said.

"Sexual relations," she said vaguely.

"How far did you go?" I demanded, an edge of rivalry in my voice.

"I think the phrase is 'all the way,' is it not?"

"You didn't!" Vivien and I shouted in unison.

"Who? Not that Dutch boy!"

"Wait. Did he ever go visit you in Iran?"

"No, he did not."

"Are we talking phone sex here?" I said. "Because technically that doesn't count."

"It happened in Switzerland."

"You mean last summer? No way."

"It was in January. My family went to Gstaad for a ski vacation. It occurred there. In a hot tub, to be specific."

"I remember you sent me a postcard." Vivien looked concerned. "Why didn't you tell us?"

"It is not exactly fit subject matter for a telegram," Shirin said, straight-faced.

This made us lose it entirely. We tried out different versions of that never-sent telegram. HOT TUB BLISS. AVALANCHE IN THE ALPS. WINTRY X-RATED ESCAPADE.

"So what happened? Was it any good?" I asked.

"Yes, it was excellent."

"Stop holding out on us, Princess." Her reticent act was getting old for my taste. We were either going to tell one another everything, or why bother? Then I realized that Shirin was more upset than she was letting on.

Her eyes filled with tears even though her expression hadn't changed.

"What happened, Shirin? Tell us. We're your friends." Vivien was always the most empathic of the three of us.

"I never saw him again." She lowered her head.

"What do you mean?"

"I don't get it," I said. "You two were serious."

"He went back to Amsterdam the next morning and that was the last I heard of him."

"Did you try calling him?" Vivien asked.

"His mother answered and requested that I not telephone him again."

"Did you write?"

"My letter was returned to me, unopened."

"That bastard!" I was ready to get on an overnight train to Holland and straighten out that son of a bitch. "We should go cut his balls off."

"I'm so sorry," Vivien said, and held Shirin's hand. They both started to cry, softly at first, then harder. It made me unbearably sad.

"Men are more trouble than they're worth," I interjected. "Why don't we just vow to become lesbians?"

At least that got them laughing again. Actually, I half meant it. If I'd had the slightest inclination toward women, I would've done it. I thought of the heartache it would save me, not to mention exponentially improving my chances for a decent mate. I wondered if lesbianism was something I could cultivate, like a taste for cigars or fine cognac. The best scenario, I figured, would be to become bisexual. That way I could double my options—and my odds. I definitely needed to think that one through.

DAY
FIVE

SHIRIN

I did not tell my friends the entire truth about Jan-Peter. Certainly I had perpetrated more shameful things in my life (breaking into a pastry shop at fourteen, for example). But somehow I could not tell them; I do not know why.

After my single encounter with Jan-Peter in the hot tub, I did not get my period for two months. It is impossible to convey the mountain of suffering I endured. This was something I could not confide to anyone, least of all my parents. Even my trusted psychiatrist, the one who had guided me through my nervous breakdown, was not privy to my anguish. Instead I sought help from strangers. I went to the back alleys of Tehran, where the herbalists and healers did brisk, black market business with ruined girls like me.

The evil old lady who sold me the killing herbs, the herbs that would ultimately abort my unborn, was filthy and untrustworthy. But I had no choice. I could not forfeit my parents' honor, my own future, to bear a child out of wedlock. How could I look my brothers in the eye? To make matters worse, I would have been forced to reveal the name of my lover—if you can call a ten-minute act by a hurried boy a lover. By law and family creed, my brothers would have had to track down Jan-Peter and kill him. Kill him, or force him to marry me. Neither option was desirable. Yes, my family was modern in most ways but on this question, the response would have been decidedly medieval.

I grew sick with worry. I barely slept and the skin around my eyes grew dark and slack. In spite of my condition, I lost weight. I had no appetite, and the little I did manage to ingest I threw up. It was not solely the nausea common to early pregnancy but a growing nausea with myself. How could I have allowed this to happen?

Endlessly I replayed the scene with Jan-Peter in my head. His earnest face. The warmth of his naked body against mine. The shiver of pleasure. That such fleeting joy could result in this ongoing nightmare seemed unthinkable. I chastised myself without mercy. There was no room in my brain except for self-recrimination. My parents feared that I was suffering another nervous breakdown. They could not fathom the nature of my problem.

After weeks of weighing various actions (at one point I thought I might hide my pregnancy from my parents and then give up the baby for adoption), I made my final decision. I went through the motions like a sleepwalker in a suit of lead.

I am not certain whether it was the herbs, or my own body, that expelled the nascent fetus. But the same evening that I drank the foul-tasting herbal tea, I began to bleed profusely. This lasted for the better part of the next day and the following night. I stayed home, complaining of a painful period (not unprecedented). I bled so much that I was terrified of hemorrhaging, but I was infinitely more terrified of revealing my secret. Going to the hospital would have been disastrous. Everyone in Tehran knew who my father was, and, by extension, who I was. In our circles, nobody remained anonymous. Although we lived in a city of millions, Tehran operated like a village. Whatever you did, good or bad—especially bad— fueled the incessant rumor mills.

Somehow I survived that horror. That is, my body survived, but my heart and my spirit were desperately wounded. This was, in part, why I returned to Switzerland again to spend time with Vivien and Ingrid. Did I dare tell them of my travails? Initially it was a relief to speak to them about my encounter with Jan-Peter. But even with them, my two dearest friends, I was ashamed to tell all. I worried, too, that those herbs had damaged me inside. My period had resumed but it was erratic and the blood had a thick, blackish cast. What if I could not have children? Would I pay for my crime with such an abominable punishment?

These incessant thoughts kept me from focusing or sleeping well. For the first time in my life, I did not excel academically. Although I continued my university mathematics courses, my other classes suffered, especially literature. I saw myself sharing the plight of every tragic heroine. In French, we read *Madame Bovary* and I nearly went mad with grief—

for her, for me, for all unhappy women. Such melodrama is not my natural inclination. Once I had been comfortably ensconced in the measurable universe, in elegant abstractions. Then, suddenly, nothing was clear to me. The world had become a murky place, overrun with impenetrable gray.

It was difficult to keep my sadness from Ingrid and Vivien, but I tried. It was somewhat easier since we had single rooms our third summer at Pierpont. Perhaps if we had been roommates again, my secret would have been impossible to guard. Besides, my friends were quite busy.

Ingrid was engrossed with her upcoming art show in Zürich. Her boyfriend—I did not like the looks of him from the start—owned a gallery there and planned to throw her a spectacular opening party, to which we were invited. I was not certain why I disapproved of him. Perhaps it was his age. Perhaps it was his sense of entitlement to the affections of a seventeen-year-old girl, even one as worldly as Ingrid. Perhaps I would have found no man suitable for my spirited friend.

The theme of Ingrid's new exhibit was "Costumes and Uniforms" and she had spent the better part of the spring taking portraits of an astonishing array of people. She explained that she wanted to explore the nature of self-representation. It was hard to reconcile this sophisticated girl with the one I had known two summers ago. In truth, she had become a star, leaving Vivien and me awestruck in her wake. When I ventured to suggest this (good-naturedly, because I genuinely wished her well), Ingrid joked that the words *delinquent* and *artist* were, in her opinion, essentially synonymous.

For her part, Vivien was preoccupied on three fronts:

1) preparing for her cooking contest at the end of the month;
2) disrupting her father's wedding to Madame Godenot;
and 3) ascertaining the whereabouts of Omar, who, Vivien
decided, she must woo back after her brutal rebuff of him
last year. I much preferred to hear about the cooking contest
than regrets over Omar or complaints about her father. Truth
be told, I was loath to hear news of any boy or man. I decided,
with grim determination, to leave the opposite sex out of my
life forever.

Vivien invited Ingrid and me to the Pierpont kitchens several times to taste her latest creations, frequently with comi-
cal results. She had a rather unfortunate series of experiments
with liver, which I detest wholeheartedly, but in the interests
of friendship I deigned to try. No amount of mustard sauces or
sautéed apricots could improve the bile-inducing meat. Ingrid,
naturally, wolfed the entire mess down without so much as a
demure burp. On the other hand, I found Vivien's desserts to
be sublime.

One day she decided to try a baked Alaska, which Chef
d'Aubigné had once deemed "a barbaric concoction by
ze cowboys." According to Vivien, he'd refused to call any
non-French chef a chef. The best he would do was call them,
sneeringly, "cooks." Anyway, Vivien decided to use a block
of Neapolitan ice cream (stealthily procured from a Pierpont
freezer) for the baked Alaska's center. She whipped up the
meringue to magnificent peaks and coated the ice-cream
block. It looked like a dowager's extravagant hairdo.

Then Vivien raised the oven temperature to quickly brown
the meringue. Ingrid and I held our breaths as she slipped the
masterpiece into the oven. But when Vivien opened the door a

few short moments later, the meringue had caught flame and her baked Alaska was a dangerous fireball. It took two aprons and a fire extinguisher—expertly wielded by Ingrid—to put out the whole dripping mess. We were fortunate not to get expelled.

How else did I entertain myself those first days of summer? I swam and rode horses (it was not the same without my Arabians but nonetheless pleasant to roam the countryside in equine company) and I studied German (a new language for me, one that would be crucial for my study of advanced sciences). Most mealtimes and evenings I spent with Ingrid and Vivien. While I could not share my deepest grief with them, their presence was a deep solace to me. We smoked and laughed, drank Ingrid's cheap wine, and gleefully plotted our revenge against Madame Godenot.

We also dreamed up our lives for decades to come. Once I had wanted to accompany my brother Cyrus across the vast, blue skies. That third summer in Switzerland, I could not say what I wanted to do anymore.

DAY
TWELVE

INGRID

My big art opening was on a Thursday night and the new headmistress, Madame Sarazin, arranged a charter bus to take the first fifty Pierpont students who signed up to my show in Zurich. You wouldn't believe the jostling and fighting and bartering that went on for those fifty spots. Madame Sarazin may have looked like somebody's grandmother but she was as hip as anyone a fraction her age. We'd definitely underestimated her—what a difference from that total nightmare, Madame Godenot, aka Vivien's future stepmother. Shit. How could this be happening to us? Vivien was hatching a desperate plot to fatten Madame Godenot to morbid obesity before the nuptials, like some pâté-destined goose. If she couldn't stop the wedding, Vivien wanted to ensure that the bride looked hideous. Shirin and I promised to go to the wedding and vowed, at minimum, to wear funereal black.

So back to my art opening. I think it would be fair to say that it started out a stellar affair, like something you'd see in a cosmopolitan European movie circa 1957. Hundreds of people showed up—not counting the busload of Pierpont girls—and many more milled outside the gallery, waiting to get in. The night was a kaleidoscope of faces, with migraine-inducing perfumes and the unmistakable smell of wealth. I was celebrated as the genius du jour, and after being an outcast for so long, it felt good to be at the white-hot center of things.

I knew my photographs were good. I'd worked hard for those shots, skipping weeks of school to wander around Toronto and the provinces to get them. Like I've said, my parents had given up trying to control me. My father was sinking deeper into his devastating memories of the war and Mutti spent her waking hours trying to keep him from falling apart. At school, the teachers threw up their hands, marked me absent, and figured I'd never graduate high school.

There was a Russian-Mexican traveling circus I followed around for awhile. I befriended hustlers and prostitutes on skid row and took their picture. I snuck into an insane asylum and photographed the patients like they were royalty, in their baby-shit green state-issued uniforms. I portrayed them with an intense dignity that made viewers question their assumptions. Finally I headed west and snapped shots of Canadian cowboys, immortalizing them.

I know how arrogant I sound. But when you believe in something, it's easy to come across as messianic. It goes with the territory. I also tried to give back whenever I could. With my trusty toolbox, I helped repair circus trailers, mended rodeo fences, fixed a balky toilet at the asylum. My mother thought I was nuts, but she had her hands full with my father and left me alone. Believe me, if I could've found a way to fix him, I would've done so.

As the opening wore on, my friends and I had a lot to drink and were on the far side of giddy. I loved having Shirin and Vivien with me, sharing in the crazy whirlwind. We started comparing notes on what people were saying. Shirin talked a Swiss couple into buying my entire series on the street hustlers of Toronto ("I told them it was seminal, revolutionary work," she said). Vivien did a hilarious imitation of a rich collector who'd called me an idiot savant. None of this could've ever happened without them, and I told them so.

"Oh, sure, you could've gotten any number of girls to pose for you naked," Vivien joked, "but they wouldn't have made you famous."

"Not to mention the cooperation of my perfectly behaved Arabian stallions," Shirin deadpanned.

"Yeah, girl, we made you who you are today!" Vivien shouted in a fake angry voice. Everyone turned to look at us, expecting a fight to break out.

I didn't know what came over us but we played our parts to the hilt, as if by some telepathic understanding.

"Okay, so what do you want?" I growled and the crowd inched away from us.

"Everything on these walls is ours!" I was surprised at how convincing Vivien sounded. *Really*, I thought, *she should go into acting if this cooking thing doesn't work out.*

"Ours!" Shirin echoed, less convincingly, but still getting into the spirit of the mock argument.

"Now, *mes cheries*, that's enough for now." It was Gerhardt with three glasses of champagne, his voice sharp. I guess he couldn't tell that we were kidding. "Drink your bubbly like nice girls. The whole world is watching."

To my complete shock, Shirin accepted the glass, then flung the champagne into Gerhardt's face. "Charlatan! Pedophile!" she accused him, and the gallery grew starkly silent. I stared at her in disbelief. Was the princess drunk?

Gerhardt turned pink as a radish. I thought he was going to slap her, he looked so livid. Instead he turned to me and with a tight voice—any tighter and he would've strangled himself—demanded: "Would you be so kind as to remove these undesirables from my gallery?"

"Who are you calling 'undesirable'?" Vivien slurred, and lunged for Gerhardt as Shirin began to laugh hysterically. He managed to dodge Vivien's attack and she landed among a few well-heeled patrons of the arts. "Oh, *excusez-moi*," she chirped, as if she hadn't just tried to clobber my boyfriend.

Gerhardt leaned over and whispered fiercely in my ear, "Now." Then he snapped his fingers, like I was some kind of lap dog.

If he hadn't snapped his fingers in that instant, the evening might've turned out a lot different. Maybe we were out of line, I'll admit that much. But nobody, and I mean nobody, messed with my friends and got away with it, much less followed up with imperious finger-snapping in my direction. In one fell swoop, my sensual lover had become a petty tyrant and an extreme undesirable himself.

"You son of a bitch." I wheeled around. "Who do you think you're ordering around?"

"This is my gallery—," he began to protest, but I cut him off.

"And these are *my* pictures." Then I turned to the crowd and shouted at the top of my lungs, "These photographs are no longer for sale here!"

"That's okay, Ingrid, we can go," Vivien said. She was entangled with some middle-aged woman in dark red lipstick who looked like a vampire bat in midmeal.

"That would be no fucking way!" I answered, and stood my ground.

"Please, *cherie*, I'm terribly sorry. Look, we've almost sold out entirely. Behold the lovely red dots." He lowered his voice so only I could hear him. "You've made a fortune here. Don't be stupid."

"Do not listen to him, Ingrid," Shirin said in her most aristocratic manner. "He is unworthy of you."

"Stay out of it, sultaness," Gerhardt hissed murderously.

"You are clearly misinformed." Shirin kept her royal gaze steady. "Perhaps we can acquaint you with the proper forms of address in my country at a more convenient time?"

"And for your information, your hors d'oeuvres are seriously substandard!" Vivien threw in for good measure. For her, this was the ultimate insult.

"Look, we're out of here," I said, and started pushing my way toward the door.

Everyone was in a quasipanic, asking how they could get their photographs, how to contact me, how much they loved my work. People were actually clinging to my arms, trying to prevent me from leaving.

"If anyone still wants their photographs," I announced, "you can reach me at the Pierpont Boarding School for

Girls." I spotted our headmistress near the entrance. "Isn't that right, Madame Sarazin?"

"Yes, of course, dear. I would certainly be happy to help you make the necessary arrangements. Now let's run along, girls. Tomorrow is a school day."

DAY
FIFTEEN

VIVIEN

I felt hungover for two days after Ingrid's art opening. What a disaster. At first we laughed over what'd happened, reliving every squalid moment, imitating one another and especially Gerhardt. But soon reality set in. Poor Ingrid was embroiled in a nasty legal suit over her photographs and her ex was bad-mouthing her all over the art world. At the rate things were going, it was doubtful she'd ever have a show in Europe again. Ingrid was alternately despondent and homicidal. Either way, it wasn't good.

After forty-eight hours on this emotional roller coaster, we convened in my room to plan a war strategy. We wanted to fight back, exact revenge, redeem Ingrid's good name—okay, maybe it wasn't so good, but we were determined to save her artistic reputation if nothing else.

"Why don't you countersue him?" I asked.

"On what basis?" Ingrid asked. She'd been drinking and smoking heavily since the opening and looked like debauchery itself.

"Breach of contract?" Shirin offered.

"We had no contract."

"So what had you agreed to, then?"

"That he would be my art dealer here," Ingrid said glumly, stabbing out a cigarette in her overflowing ashtray. "He gave his word. And now we know how good *that* was. Look, I just want my fucking photographs back. I'll sell them in Shanghai, if I have to."

"I am quite certain there are no art galleries there," Shirin said. "Since the Cultural Revolution, artists and intellectuals have been sent to the countryside to—"

"Thank you, Walter Cronkite," Ingrid said, cutting her off.

"Who is Walter Cronkite?"

"Jesus. Never mind."

"Newscaster. Let's move on," I interjected. "We have to think creatively here. Gerhardt has a lot of money and connections, and he's a lot older than us so—"

"Stop right there," Shirin ordered. She jumped to her feet and started pacing the room. "You just said the magic words, Vivi."

"Money?"

"A lot older."

"Yeah, so what?" Ingrid was struggling to remove the cork from another wine bottle, a German gewürztraminer, she informed us. She was branching out from the reds. She poured us each a Dixie cup full.

"How old are you, Ingrid?" Shirin persisted.

"What kind of stupid question is that? You know how old I am."

"Exactly."

"I don't get it."

"You are only seventeen. A mere girl. Underage."

"You're not suggesting—," I began.

"That is precisely what I am suggesting."

"I still don't get it," Ingrid polished off three cups of wine in quick succession. "Hmm, this stuff's not bad at all."

"Listen, Ingrid," I insisted. "You're under eighteen and Gerhardt is, like, fifty years old. I mean, the guy's ancient. You could sue him for corrupting a minor."

At this point, we couldn't help laughing. The idea of Ingrid being corrupted by anyone was a stretch, much less her being a *minor* anything. Maybe that was why this hadn't occurred to us before.

"Oh, that's rich," Ingrid said, cracking up. "I've got a rap sheet longer than Santa's bad-girl list. Besides, this is Europe. It's the seventies. Everyone's been screwing everyone else since they were fourteen."

"That may be true," Shirin conceded. "But you can take him to court in Canada where the laws, I presume, are not so lenient."

"Yeah, well, that's where everyone and their brother knows me, too."

"It might be worth a try," I offered. "You've got nothing to lose. And the publicity from the trial might incite a burst of public sympathy."

"Or notoriety," Shirin said. "In any case, your reputation will be secured. It will not matter what Gerhardt says after you disgrace him in court."

"People will be clamoring for your work," I said.

"This will drive the prices up," Shirin insisted. "Especially for the photographs in question. They will become a precious commodity. That is how the oil ministers in my country arrange our profits."

"So that's why gas prices are skyrocketing?"

"Precisely. You could also write to the *New York Times*, apprising them of the delicacy of your situation."

"The fucking president of the United States is getting impeached," Ingrid whined. "Why would anyone care about me? Besides, I'm going to be eighteen in two months."

"Then we must work with alacrity," Shirin said.

"What the hell does that mean?" Ingrid was growing cranky.

"Fast!" I yelled, attempting a lame victory dance.

"Okay, okay." Ingrid shook her head even as she was agreeing with us. "But I want to nail him right here in Switzerland. Shit in his backyard. We'll ruin the son of a bitch."

We barely heard our housekeeper's knocking amidst our revelry. Babette lived in the servants' quarters down the hall. An inveterate gossip, she was known as an effective go-between for Swiss boarding school lovers. For a price, of course.

"*Bon soir.* Eh, I have a message for Mademoiselle Vivien from a young man, *trés beau.*" Then she handed me a letter in a thick, sky blue envelope.

For a minute my heart stopped. With all the tumult of the last few days, I'd nearly forgotten about Omar. I'd sent word to Le Rosey through reliable channels, i.e., Babette, that I wanted to see him again. Until now, I'd heard nothing back. The housekeeper stood there, awaiting compensation. I dug in my pockets but came up with just a few centimes. Shirin came to the rescue with a fifty-franc note, which she pulled from her change purse. With a discreet flourish, she handed it to Babette.

Transaction *complét.*

I held the envelope in my hands, turning it over and over, running my fingers along the script on the front.

"Open the damn thing already." Ingrid tried to snatch the envelope.

"Give her time," Shirin intervened. "This is an important moment in Vivi's romantic history. We must allow her the space she needs."

"From legal crusader to guru in one fell swoop," Ingrid said, rolling her eyes.

I hadn't been to a church or a synagogue in years, but I closed my eyes and fervently prayed. *Please, please, let it be good news. Please, please, give me another chance with him.* My hands trembled as I opened the envelope, bracing for the worst. I recognized the handwriting immediately—it was Omar's—but I couldn't focus my eyes to read the words. Maybe the whole thing was a terrible delusion on my part. Ingrid lost patience and grabbed the letter. As I stood there, anxious and stiff-spined, she read aloud.

My dearest Vivien,

I have not forgotten you. How could I? But I decided, this time, to avoid the thorny rose trellis and ask you to meet me outside. I am waiting for you by the front gate. Will you come?

Yours,

Omar

There was a moment of silence as the words sunk in. Then we started shrieking and running around like banshees. It was time to get to work. Shirin and Ingrid picked out my clothes (pretty sundress, pink cashmere sweater), combed my hair (down, side part), made me brush my teeth twice, and spritzed me with precious tuberose perfume from Iran. They escorted me as far as the front door of Pierpont's dormitory, taking turns giving me a hug. My legs felt rubbery and weak and my heart was hammering so hard I thought it would crash through my chest.

"Ready?" they asked, glowing with happiness for me.

"Ready," I said, and walked out the door to meet Omar.

It took a few minutes for my eyes to adjust to the dark as I stumbled along the gravel driveway. There was no moon but the sky had a faint green tinge, as if it were trying to absorb the earth's flora. The air *smelled* green, too.

Omar was better-looking than I remembered him, as impossible as that sounds. And he was carrying a bouquet of long-stemmed roses.

"In memory of our last meeting." Omar smiled, offering me the bouquet.

This guy was too good to be true. I felt guilty and scared and embarrassed all at once. I wanted to apologize for my behavior last year. I wanted to say he was so damn handsome that he'd scared the hell out of me. I wanted to tell him that I was afraid to get my heart broken and end up miserable like my parents. Plus I was growing dizzy from the intense fragrance of the roses and the whole blooming garden.

Nothing came out of my mouth. I stood there stupidly, staring into his face, when a butterfly landed on his shoulder. It was pale blue with gold edging and it opened and closed its wings once before flying away. Soundlessly I pointed at it but the butterfly merged with the night before Omar could see it.

Omar looked into my eyes and read my confusion.

"I promise I won't hurt you, Vivien."

He reached for my hand and it felt warm and moist, like the first time he took it at the garden party two summers ago. Omar wasn't that shy, chubby boy anymore, but I wasn't sure how much I'd changed, or if I'd changed at all. Then he leaned toward me, his lips grazing mine so softly that it tickled, and I began to giggle. Then we kissed again, harder this time, and I knew, at last, that I might love him.

DAY
SEVENTEEN

SHIRIN

It seemed that life was happening to everyone but me our third summer in Switzerland. I had undergone a terrible ordeal but nobody knew about it. Was a life lived in private, I wondered, any less worthy than a noisy, public one? I agonized over whether to tell Vivien and Ingrid about the abortion. But in my shame I stayed silent, hoping that my pain would diminish with time. Ingrid and Vivien did not seem to notice my distress those first weeks at Pierpont. There was too much otherwise absorbing my friends. I did not blame them. Alone in my room at night, I cried until I drifted off into a restless sleep. Often I awoke with the name of my unborn child on my lips, an imaginary boy I named Cyrus, after my beloved brother.

As a girl, I had never believed in imaginary friends. I scoffed at my cousins who entertained such childishness and refused to engage in their pointless games. Yet there I was, years later, doing precisely what I had derided.

My suffering took a bizarre turn. Naturally I was relieved that I would not suffer the shame of bearing a child out of wedlock, and I was physically and emotionally depleted by the ordeal. You must believe this: If I could have, I would have banished the memory forever.

Yet I found myself obsessed with my unborn boy. I do not know why, but I imagined that he was a boy. I found myself continuously talking to him, murmuring in his tiny, shelled ear. I imagined bathing him, taking care to wash every sweet crevice of his body, then sprinkling him with rose-scented talcum powder. This was madness, a dreadful torture, but I could not stop these reveries. I had expelled the baby from my body but I could not expel him from my mind.

Time had no meaning in my daydreams. I saw my boy on his first day of school, his navy knee socks rolled up to his dimpled knees. Under my father's guidance, I watched him riding his first horse, the gentlest of our Arabians, with polished boots and a hand-woven leather riding crop. I laughed when he tasted his first pomegranate, spitting out the bitter seeds. And I indulged him his favorite snack: crushed pistachios drizzled with honey.

Many unaccountable hours elapsed as I indulged in such fanciful musings. It was impossible for me to reconcile the fact that I would never get to know this boy, lost to me forever by my own cowardly actions. I churned through my studies mechanically, as I would any distasteful task. Only the company of my cherished friends permitted me a respite from my brooding. With them, at least, I could have a bit of fun.

It was the arrival of a telegram from my brother that put a stop, if temporarily, to my reveries. Cyrus had managed to secure a furlough from the Iranian Air Force to visit me in Switzerland. He said he would stay at a hotel in Rolle, and promised to take me out to fattening dinners every night until I grew as plump as a partridge (his words). I do not know what my parents told Cyrus about my dispiriting spring. It was not easy for him to leave the Air Force, notwithstanding our connections to the shah. No matter. Cyrus would be coming in a week, and I was eager for him to arrive.

The afternoon I received his telegram, I headed straight to the Pierpont kitchens with my news. This was where Vivien spent every spare minute she was not with Omar (their reunion had been a great success). She was working diligently on her menu for the culinary competition in Lausanne. I discovered her with eight burners on high and myriad experiments in the oven. She was debating between designing a classic European menu or a series of experimental New World dishes.

No sooner did I walk through the door than she thrust a wooden spoon heaped with Coquille Saint Jacques at me.

"Please, Shirin, try this for me, will you? Is the cream sauce too gluey? Tell me what you really think. Don't hold back."

I was not a reliable fan of scallops but I opened my mouth just the same. Vivien looked on the verge of a nervous breakdown. I certainly recognized the symptoms: wild eyes, disheveled appearance, compressed and frantic speech, sweat beading along the hairline, a palpable sense of desperation.

"Mmm. The consistency of the sauce is fine," I said, taking a moment to savor it. "But I think it could use a touch of salt."

"Oh my God, I completely forgot the salt!"

Vivien busied herself refilling the grinder, then subjected her scallops to a miniature hailstorm of sea salt. She stirred the concoction with the same wooden spoon, tasted it, and then offered it to me once more.

"Perfect," I pronounced, and it was—delicate and refined, truly delicious. She was most gifted in the kitchen.

"What about this?" Vivien practically assaulted me with another spoon, this one filled with a bright, saffron-colored sauce.

One taste made me reel back in shock. My eyes began to water and my tongue and throat were radiating heat. My lips tingled violently, like when a limb goes prickly from prolonged immobility—except that my reaction was more severe.

"Are you planning to kill the judges?" I rasped, running to the faucet for water.

"Don't drink water! It'll only make it worse." Vivien apologized, offering me a stack of what turned out to be homemade corn tortillas. This calmed the burning somewhat, though I was not sure what remained of my taste buds.

"I'm so sorry, Shirin. I thought you were accustomed to spicy foods in Iran."

"I am not sure how you got that impression," I mumbled, madly stuffing the corn tortillas in my mouth (quite tasty, in fact). I could feel my body temperature rising alarmingly. "Is that a sauce or a secret weapon?"

"Both," Vivien said with a laugh. Then she grew serious. "I don't know which way to go in this contest. If I cook what everyone else is cooking, I won't stand out. Any decent chef can whip up a great béchamel sauce. But who around here can make fantastic carnitas?"

"Well, this sauce will surely make you stand out," I said, attempting to talk while simultaneously aerating my tongue. "But I am not sure this is the attention you wish to seek. What do you call it, anyway?"

"Red chile sauce. It goes on all sorts of Mexican dishes."

"Well, perhaps you can offer it to your competitors?" I suggested in jest.

"Yeah, I'd win by default." Vivien rubbed her hands in a diabolical manner.

"But you might be disqualified—"

"For murder?"

"Perhaps they would hold your place in cooking school during your sojourn in prison?"

"Or until I broke out!" Vivien was enjoying the fantasy. "You could bring me a nail file hidden in a birthday cake, like in those old chain-gang movies."

"Count on me," I said, and laughed along with her. But, in spite of my best intentions, my laughter soon turned to tears. Once I started, I could not stop.

"Shirin, what's wrong? Is the chile still burning your tongue?"

Everything I had kept inside me for so long erupted like an enormous wave. "I had a baby!" I cried. My body was shaking and it was impossible to form any more words. Vivien dropped her spoon and looked at me, wide-eyed.

"What do you mean?" she asked, gently wrapping her arms around me.

She put her face so close to mine that I could see the vein pulsing in her temple. She was sympathy and concern, confusion and dismay.

What else dare I tell her?

"I did not have a baby, but I almost did." I broke into another round of sobs. "What I mean to say is—"

"It's okay, Shirin. You can tell me."

Vivien's voice was low and soothing and she stroked my hair, wiped the tears from my cheeks. She could have been my mother. The thought of this idea made me cry harder. Vivien began rocking me, humming softly. Later, she told me it was a Cuban lullaby that her Tía Cuca used to sing to her at bedtime, or when Vivien woke up with nightmares about another bomb planted under the family car. The singing calmed me in that universal way of lullabies. And I was infinitely grateful for Vivien's tenderness. It was more than my own mother could have offered me.

It was her tenderness that freed me to tell Vivien the whole story—about my brief pregnancy, about the dirty back-alley herbalist, about my near hemorrhaging, my shame, and my unceasing grief and solitude. I told her about the baby boy I imagined never having and with whom I spoke every day, about his capacity for forgiveness and my own inability to forgive myself. I told Vivien that I wanted nothing more than to bring this lost boy back, this baby Cyrus, to have him cry out with life and grace mine forever. I wanted this, or to forget him completely. Anything but my continual torment.

Vivien listened to me the whole time without saying a word, her eyes fixed on mine, her hands alternately shielding and rubbing my back. When I was done, and spent, and exhausted beyond anything I'd ever experienced, she told me she loved me.

DAY
TWENTY

INGRID

It wasn't exactly the summer I'd been planning. I hadn't
expected to be swamped in a lawsuit over *my own photographs*
with a former lover. I hadn't expected to be more heartbroken
than I could let on, even with my best friends. I hadn't expected
that this fiasco would shut down my creativity in a big way. Nor
had I expected to get as depressed as I got, to the point that
I could hardly get out of bed. Least of all, I hadn't expected
my father to show up at the Pierpont Boarding School for Girls
completely out of the blue one Friday morning, looking for me.

What did Vati want? For me to accompany him on a tour
of Germany's concentration camps. You heard me correctly.
For thirty years, my father had refused to set foot on European
soil. He'd broken that record by picking us up from Pierpont
that first summer, but he'd assured us that he had no inten-

tion of returning. In fact, he'd vowed to stay away from the Old World altogether. He hadn't wanted to face the horrific destruction and delusions of his country's past, and the part he'd played in it.

His last "involvement," as he once referred to it, took place during the Warsaw ghetto uprising. I didn't know what he had, or hadn't, done. All I knew was that whatever had happened there had finally made him leave Germany for good. It took him two years, four languages, one arrest, and every penny he could beg, borrow, or steal to make it to Canada.

Vati never looked back. At least, not until he got in that car accident in the cornfield and started having nightmares. Then all he could do was look back. Why my father decided he had to get to the bottom of his past in the middle of *my* crisis, I didn't understand. Frankly, it was not something I wanted to explore. At least not then. There was enough going on without his drama. Why couldn't he just focus on the damn present, and refrain from dragging me into his mess? It wasn't like he'd invited my mother or sister to go along with him. Vati insisted that I alone needed to participate in his gruesome journey. It was the last thing I wanted to do.

For once, I wanted to get through a summer in Switzerland without being kicked out or universally loathed. Was that remotely possible? What was it about me that attracted constant mayhem? I was a lightning rod for chaos. Whatever it was, I was getting sick and tired of it. It wasn't that I didn't appreciate a fair degree of excitement. But there comes a point when things can get too fucking exhausting. And I'd reached that point.

I wanted things to work out for a change. Was it too much

to ask to have a father who didn't show up in the middle of my summer and demand that I accompany him on a goddamn spiritual quest? Look, the only thing working for me that July was my friendship with Vivien and Shirin. Or at least I thought it was working. They'd been hanging out a lot together, tête-à-tête, in deep conversations that excluded me. I didn't pay much attention at first because I was caught up in my own misery. But soon, I suspected, even our friendship would be sorely tested.

VIVIEN

I was in a serious bind. Shirin had begged me not to tell a soul about her abortion. That, of course, included Ingrid. To make matters worse, Shirin confided that her periods were coming out black and putrid and twice as often as they should, like she was rotting inside. She desperately needed to see a doctor, but she wouldn't hear of it. Maybe she'd poisoned herself with those crazy herbs and was dying a slow death. If I didn't insist that she get help—and something awful happened to her—I'd never forgive myself.

I thought of telling her brother when he came to visit. According to Shirin, nobody understood her better, or loved her more. But when I suggested this, she burst into tears and made me swear on the lives of everyone I hold dear that I would never, ever, breathe a word of her "disgrace" to her brother.

Compounding the stress were two things: First, I was officially going out with Omar, which was a good thing but still stressful. Second, I was driving myself and everyone around me crazy over the culinary competition. It would be held during my last weekend at Pierpont, ruining any possibility of end-of-summer fun. I would've preferred if the organizers had rounded up all the aspiring chefs without warning, put us in a well-supplied kitchen, and said *You have three hours to come up with a meal. May the best chef win.* Competition over.

Instead I was putting myself, and everyone around me, through agony. I needed to win. If I won, I thought, it would prove to my parents that I could skip college and go straight to cooking school. I wasn't a bad student, but my heart wasn't in biology, or American history, or, God forbid, algebra. I wanted to be a professional chef and I didn't want to waste time getting there.

Over the summer, I'd concocted a half-dozen extravagant menus for the competition but none that I felt confident about. I was tempted to go all-out ethnic, feature Oaxacan mole made with thirty-seven ingredients. But I suspected that the judges wanted contestants to showcase their solid continental training. Did the world really need a better beef bourguignonne, or a more perfect profiterole?

As if all this weren't enough . . . overshadowing everything was the impending, unspeakable wedding of my father to Madame Godenot.

Omar was incredibly understanding about all these pressures. He lavishly praised my culinary experiments, complaining only about how much weight he was gaining. He was as beautiful as ever, except for a pimply breakout on his forehead, probably due to the rich foods I was force feeding him. What I wanted to tell him most—Shirin's sad story—I had to keep to myself. Omar seemed to know whenever I was thinking about her because he'd say, "You have that faraway look again, Vivien. What's on your mind?"

I could usually distract him with kisses. We kissed for hours, losing all track of time. I don't know how we managed to kiss for so long. It didn't occur to either of us to get a hotel room, or to go any further than we did.

There was a lot going on in the world beyond our lives at Pierpont. The Watergate hearings were dragging on but none of us paid much attention to them. There was a coup in Chile and an OPEC oil embargo and the U.S. was bombing Cambodia but these barely registered on our radar. The headlines came to us from the TV lounge at Pierpont or the occasional newspaper, as if from another planet. The truth was that we were much too wrapped up in our own worlds to notice.

DAY TWENTY-TWO

SHIRIN

Vivien and Ingrid came with me to meet Cyrus in his hotel dining room. I hadn't seen my brother since Christmas and I was both elated and nervous to see him. So much had happened in the intervening months. A universe of change. I prayed he would not be able to tell what had transpired by looking at me.

When we were children, or, rather, when I was a child and Cyrus was an adolescent, we used to play a game called Read My Mind. We would sit facing each other, eyes wide open, and try to "read" what the other was thinking. I rarely guessed correctly, although he laughed when I repeatedly tried the generic "girls." Cyrus, on the other hand, always knew what was on my mind. One might attribute it to common sense, or a particular sensitivity—certainly nothing scientific—but my brother read me discomfortingly well.

Vivien and Ingrid had heard me talk so much about my brother that they were eager to meet him. Ingrid jokingly suggested that we exchange salutes instead of handshakes, and wondered whether an Iranian Air Force pilot might "take out," as she put it, "a scummy, soon-to-be ex–art dealer." At the other extreme, Vivien worried whether the hotel food would be good enough for him and suggested that we plan to leave after the appetizers if they did not prove satisfactory.

My brother was staying at the poshest hotel in Rolle, an ornate nineteenth-century building facing Lake Geneva, festooned with flags from every canton in Switzerland. It was the middle of the night, Tehran time, when we finally met him in the velvety, cavernous lobby. Cyrus looked handsome in his linen suit and blue silk shirt—tall and muscular, with thickly lashed eyes and a wonderful smile. He was growing a mustache, which was not terribly attractive in my opinion, but gave him the air of a younger Omar Sharif.

I ran to him and we held each other tight, not saying a word. When he tried to look me full in the face, I turned away and introduced him to my friends. It took me a moment to register what their expressions betrayed. Their jaws were unhinged and their eyes blinked in surprise. It was as though they wanted to reprimand me: *We cannot believe you were holding out on us about your stunningly gorgeous brother.*

Dinner was awkward at first, with platitudes dominating the conversation. Soon we banished them, or, rather, Ingrid did. She could not make small talk if you paid her a king's ransom.

"So, what do you do for sex in the Air Force?" Ingrid asked nonchalantly, popping an olive into her mouth.

Cyrus lowered his eyes, then cleared his throat before looking back at Ingrid. He had not appreciated the question.

Vivien started choking on *her* olive and tried to change the subject.

"I understand the shah is striving to rapidly modernize Iran. What are the opportunity costs of doing so?"

"I can see you're well informed, Mademoiselle Wahl," Cyrus answered.

"Please, call me Vivien." She blushed the color of the red pepper purée on the table, which was offered to us as an alternative to butter.

"There is a tremendous amount of controversy over the approach the shah has taken. It seems to benefit those who are already rich at the expense of the poor." Cyrus stopped and grinned broadly. "But enough politics for now. I understand from Shirin that you are a superb chef. I'm an amateur cook myself but I know a fair amount about Persian cuisine. Are you familiar with our chicken in pomegranate sauce?"

"Shirin never mentioned it." Vivien shot me a quizzical look.

"Perhaps I can teach it to you during my brief stay in Switzerland?"

"Oh, I'd love that. I mean, yes, that would be very nice. I'm trying to figure out a menu for a cooking contest next week and I'm still not sure what to prepare."

"I can assure you that this chicken, if done properly, will win over the judges. It is food for the soul—and the heart."

"Ingrid is an extraordinary photographer," I jumped in, noticing that our Canadian friend was getting restless at best, and on the verge of rudeness at worst. Ingrid needed to be the center of attention. This was not one of her finer traits.

"Is that so?" Cyrus said, perusing his menu. "This is a definite improvement over the institutional food I've grown accustomed to. Could you please help me choose, Vivien? I'm at the mercy of your culinary expertise."

"Uh, our little chef here already has a boyfriend," Ingrid blurted out.

Vivien and I stared at her in disbelief. What in God's name was she doing?

"As a matter of fact, she's supposed to be meeting him right now. A Tunisian hunk with a big bank account. They spend most nights making out along the waterfront. Really, it's quite a spectacle. Everyone in town is talking about it."

"Oh?" Cyrus did his best to ignore her. "Would you recommend the trout this time of year, Vivien?"

But Vivien had been rendered speechless by Ingrid's outburst.

"You know, I think I'll go meet up with him right now and tell him you're indisposed," Ingrid continued, lighting a cigarette. "As a favor to you, Vivien. This way, you don't have to tell him that you're dumping him for Shirin's brother." She blew the smoke out of her mouth with such force that it looked like a mushroom cloud over our heads.

"Ingrid, perhaps you have had too much to drink?" I ventured.

"Don't make excuses for me, Princess. I'm perfectly sober. Too damn sober, in fact."

"Then you do not have an excuse." I am not inclined to violence but I wanted to slap her. "I suggest that you go this instant."

"Oh, you can't get rid of me so easily. What are you going to do? Throw me in one of the shah's prisons? Don't you stick dissidents in burlap sacks with hungry cats?" She bolted back the red wine she had ordered. "See? I'm well informed too."

"She's had a very stressful summer," Vivien interjected, trying to save the situation.

I was impressed with Vivien's unfailing kindness, as was my brother. He told me later that he admired her character at that moment.

"Come on, Ingrid." Vivien stood up and took Ingrid's arm. "I think we should get you back to school. You're exhausted and I know you didn't mean what you said."

Ingrid did not expect this and stood up like an automaton. Already I could tell she was feeling remorse. Ingrid was vicious in an unbridled fight but collapsed, utterly, in the face of pure goodness.

Then, with a sheepish wave, Vivien led the chagrined Ingrid out of the restaurant.

DAY
TWENTY-FOUR

INGRID

I was beyond mortified and didn't want to see anyone. How could I have done that to my closest friends? Scratch that. To my only true friends in the world. I said I was sorry about a million times. While it mollified Vivien and, to a lesser extent, Shirin, it did nothing to calm me down. Everything was shit and everything I tried only made things shittier. I decided, as a last resort, to go with my father to the concentration camp he so desperately wanted to visit—to Dachau, just outside his home-town of Munich. How much worse could it get?

The train ride there was interminable, a far cry from my hopeful attempt at adventure the summer before. That first trip to Munich had set me on an artistic course without my realizing it. All I'd done was walk around the city and go to a few museums, but something must've shifted inside me. A

brush with the motherland and suddenly I'd found my calling as a photographer—at least, this was the story I kept
telling everyone. But what'd started promisingly had ended
in a big, fat mess. It seemed to me that that's what I was
really good at.

Uncharacteristically, my father tried to take an interest in
me. He asked me a hundred questions that I had no intention
of answering. I wanted to tell him that it was too late for us
to start bonding, that he shouldn't bother. He'd spent years
away from home selling his stupid fans, ignoring the bedlam
at home, trying to wish it away. I didn't care if he wanted to
make amends now. What I wanted was to get the whole damn
trip over with and have him leave me alone.

"Tell me about your friends, *liebchen*," Vati insisted.

No answer from me. It was awkward as hell sitting on the
train with my father for so many hours. It made me realize,
too, that I'd actually never taken a good look at him. Strong
jawed and well built, without too many wrinkles for a man
his age. I wondered what he'd looked like in his youth—his
fucking Nazi youth.

"They seem like nice girls."

"Nice, sure." I turned and looked out the window. The
countryside was speeding by so fast it looked like a blurry
quilt. How did people make a living off these toy dairy farms?
Even the cows looked like miniature windup toys. I'd brought
my camera with me and was half tempted to take a few shots
through the window, to capture the essence of speed, of tran-
sience. But I couldn't explain this to my father.

"Your sister sends her regards."

"You told me that already."

"She's in England again this summer." Vati took off his glasses and meticulously wiped them clean with his spotless handkerchief.

"Jesus, I know that too. Our tennis prodigy. Do you think I'm completely oblivious to what goes on in our family?"

My father finished cleaning his glasses, taking extra care with the rims, then carefully placed them back on his nose. His eyes grew larger and bluer behind the lenses. "As a matter of fact, I do."

That shut down the conversation for a while.

It was late afternoon by the time we got to Munich. Vati rented a car near the train station for the drive to Dachau. He looked tired and defeated, and, against my own instincts, I began feeling sorry for him. Something about his patient bearing toward me softened me up, if only slightly. I tried to imagine what it must be like for him to endure the hideous torment of his past. The guilt of participating in unspeakable crimes, of not fighting back. Of fleeing the scene to where no one could find him, point an accusing finger, and shout "Murderer!"

Then I thought of how my sufferings were pretty meager in comparison. Damn it, perspective was the last thing I needed. I wanted to wallow in my misery.

"You look beat, Vati," I said in my kindest voice. "Why don't you let me drive?"

My father gazed at me with such gratitude that I thought he was going to cry. This nearly made me rescind the offer. I'd never seen my father cry. I didn't know what I'd do if he started. I wanted to avoid this scenario at all costs.

I stayed in the far right lane of the autobahn heading northwest out of the city. Believe me, I'm not a squeamish driver, but to travel on a German roadway is to take your life in your hands. It's weird how people can be so stiff and decorous in one context, and turn into homicidal maniacs in another. I swear there were drivers going 150 miles per hour, a fair number of them old ladies.

Dachau looked like any other German town, with its well-tended square and homes and flower boxes spilling over with geraniums. Most of the shops were closed but there were a couple of pubs open. Who could've guessed that the whole system of mass extermination had begun right here, on the edge of this innocent-looking burg? I'd learned in history class that Dachau was the oldest of the concentration camps, opened in the early thirties when Hitler needed more room to house his increasingly long list of undesirables. My father would've barely been a teenager when it opened.

There weren't many people on the streets but I took note of everybody's age. If they appeared old enough to have lived through World War II, I wondered; *Where were you when they were burning the Jews? Did you hear their cries at night? Did you profit from a little business with the camp? Assist with the so-called medical experiments? Perhaps you turned a blind eye? Deafened your ears? Went about your chores pretending you didn't smell the acrid smoke of human flesh from the concentration camp's chimneys?*

"Drive over that way," my father instructed.

Vati seemed to know his way around. I followed where he pointed, which led us to the front gates of Dachau. With its welcoming stolid arches and peeling paint, it might've been the once grand entrance to some neglected castle gardens, a place to stroll with children or ride bicycles on a fine spring Sunday. I turned off the motor and sat there next to my father, breathing in the same warm summer air, faintly fragrant with roses. I sat there wordlessly, breathing in his memories.

"Do you know this place?" I finally asked him, my voice hoarse.

His eyes filled with tears as he whispered back, "Yes."

Neither of us said anything for a long time. A couple of crows raised a fuss in a gigantic elm tree. Their cries seemed to echo for miles. I stole a glance at my father and felt the weight of his history bearing down on him, on us both.

"I worked here," he said, choking on the words. "I did unspeakable things."

I didn't want to imagine what he meant. I forced my mind to go blank, to fill with white noise. I didn't want his nightmares to become mine.

"I was a boy." Vati wiped away a tear that had trickled to the edge of his chin. "A mere boy." He pulled a handkerchief from his pocket and buried his face in it. Then his sobs began, wracking, inconsolable. There was nothing I could do but watch. When he emerged from his handkerchief, his face was ugly and swollen, like someone had punched him.

"I will make no excuses." My father tried to steady his voice. "I will make no excuses, Ingrid. But I must tell you what happened. Will you listen?"

He took my hand, squeezed it hard. I wanted to pull it from his grip but I didn't. I sat there. I sat there with my father in front of the gates of Dachau, and listened.

DAY TWENTY-SIX

VIVIEN

Ingrid's father and mine practically ran into each other on the front steps of Pierpont. Mr. Baum was returning with Ingrid from their concentration camp trip. It was strange the way he and Papi shook hands and eyed each other, like they'd met before but couldn't quite place where. I wondered if Ingrid had told her father about mine. How he'd suffered during World War II and barely escaped with his life. I hadn't told Papi about Ingrid's dad having been a Nazi. I was afraid that he'd forbid me from having anything to do with her.

My father had shown up unannounced, ostensibly to support me during my upcoming culinary battle in Lausanne. I didn't trust his explanation so Papi quickly confessed the real reason for his sudden appearance: he and Madame Godenot had broken off their engagement. I kept very still, not quite believing what he'd said. Inside, I was jumping up and down with excitement.

Papi suggested that we go out to dinner so he could fill me in. I could tell he was very distracted and I wondered if he was thinking about Mr. Baum. We chose a simple café in the heart of Rolle. It was a relief not to have to worry about cooking, or even fine dining, for one solitary evening. We ordered quiche Lorraine and salads and mugs of café au laits. Papi was on the subdued side for the first ten minutes, probably trying to figure out what he should tell me.

"Where would you like me to begin?" he asked, shrugging his shoulders.

"Start with the breakup." I tried to tamp down any hint of triumph in my voice.

Papi looked miserable. His eyes were darkly pouched and he'd lost about twenty pounds. His fingers continuously drummed on the table, or played with his unused soup spoon. A part of me secretly relished his misery. He'd made my mother and me suffer immeasurably these past couple of years. Now it was his turn. Somehow I didn't feel as satisfied as I'd imagined.

"Short version or long?" he asked forlornly.

"Give me the headline first, then tell me the whole story."

"Wayward husband sees estranged wife and falls in love with her all over again."

"You saw Mom?" I felt nervous, like a bird was fluttering inside me.

"Inadvertently. She was eating dinner with her new boyfriend. I happened to be walking by and saw them in a restaurant window on Madison and Seventy-sixth. At first, I couldn't believe it was her."

"She's changed a lot." I was shocked but tried not to show it.

"It was more than just her appearance. She looked alive, vivacious, and she was clearly enjoying herself. I hadn't seen her enjoying herself in so long that I thought it wasn't possible anymore. Perhaps it was me who'd killed her joy. In any case, she was radiantly happy and I remembered how we, too, had been radiantly happy once. I wanted to reclaim that, to reclaim her."

"What did you do?" I put down my fork. "You didn't barge in on them, did you?" I pictured my father muscling his way to their table and telling that investment banker bozo to hit the road.

"No, I managed to control myself." He smiled ruefully. "But I knew from that moment forward that I wanted your mother back. I had to break the news to Margot. Needless to say, it wasn't an easy task."

"What did she—"

"I'll spare you the details, Vivien—and no small amount of schadenfreude. Do you know what that means?"

"Dad, it's the lifeline of gossip. Of course I know what it means."

"I see." He didn't look amused.

"So then what happened?"

"I began sending your mother flowers. Flowers and more flowers. Long-stemmed roses and hothouse orchids, lilies from every corner of the world. You name it, I sent it. I don't know whether it was the collective, asphyxiating scent of those thousands of blooms that made her reconsider—"

"She said yes?" I interrupted, impatient. This would be too good to be true.

He held up his hand, wanting to finish.

"—Or perhaps it was the accompanying bad poetry I wrote that moved her, or, more likely, elicited her pity—"

"You wrote Mom poetry?" I was incredulous. My business-man father writing poetry was more than I could wrap my mind around.

"I did." He looked slightly embarrassed, then defiant. "And why not, may I ask?"

"Okay, Dad. So you wrote poetry. Are you guys back together again, or what?"

"Not yet. But she did agree to meet me for coffee. That was last week."

"How did it go?" I felt my chest constricting. I wasn't sure I wanted to hear everything after all.

"Well, let's say that I impressed her with my sincerity and my ardor."

"But she wasn't buying it?"

"Not quite. That's where I was hoping you could help."

"Me? How?"

"By expressing your desire to see us back together. By insisting to your mother that she give me another chance."

Papi looked at me so intently and hopefully that a lot of my anger toward him dissipated. But not entirely. My mother was probably wondering if she could trust him again after every-thing he'd done. I was thinking the same thing. Maybe he needed to suffer our absence a little longer, realize what he'd given up chasing those other women, not to mention humili-ating me in public with the headmistress. Maybe he was just jealous. Maybe as soon as he had her, he'd be off again. That would be heinous.

"But first," Papi continued, "I must ask your forgiveness."

"It wasn't easy watching you—"

"I know, *mi amor*. Please forgive me my selfishness. It was as though I were living in a bright tunnel, blinded by my own—"

"Fine, Dad. But how do we know it won't happen again?"

"I can't answer that for you. All I can say is that I can't live in the shadow of your absence anymore. Nor that of your mother. It's too painful, and lonely. My distant past with Margot was a mirage—"

"I don't really want to hear about her," I snapped, my anger renewed.

"Please, *hija*. Believe me when I say that I've suffered without you and your mother, that I want us under one roof."

Neither of us ate anything more and we didn't bother ordering dessert. I wanted to forgive my father, but I couldn't do it on my mother's behalf. That was something they'd have to work out by themselves. Papi reached across the table. His hand was warm and slightly calloused, and it firmly held mine.

After dinner we took a long walk along Lake Geneva as dusk lingered in the summer sky, flamboyant with streaks of fuchsia and orange. I missed Omar and wished that I could introduce him to my father. Omar knew the whole story about the headmistress, but I still wanted him to like my dad. When I told Papi about Omar, he wasn't even upset.

"I'm glad you've found someone who loves you, *mi amor*."

"You're okay with it?"

"*Pero claro*. You're a wonderful girl. Why wouldn't someone be crazy about you?"

"A lot of parents would be worried and—"

"Would you prefer that I prohibit you from seeing him?"

"Uh, no."

"Then I trust your judgment. When will I get to meet him?"

"Tonight, if you want. He's coming over later."

When we got back to Pierpont, Ingrid and her father were waiting for us on the front steps. Papi looked agitated but I wasn't sure why.

"May I have a word with you, Mr. Wahl?" Ingrid's father asked softly.

"What's it about?" Papi looked around him, as if searching for an escape route. The sweat was visible on his forehead, dampening his neck.

"*Bitte.* I must know."

Papi followed Ingrid's father toward the copse of willow trees on the far side of the expansive lawn. There was a gazebo and it was favorite meeting place for trysts. It was weird seeing the two of them walk over there together.

To complicate things, Omar chose that exact moment to speed up in his brand-new Fiat convertible. It was bright orange and looked dazzlingly dangerous. I wanted to jump in and fly away to anywhere but here. The car sputtered to a stop.

"What's going on?" Omar asked, kissing me on the cheek.

"Our fathers were lovers in another life," Ingrid cracked and Omar's eyes widened.

"Jesus, Ingrid."

"Respectability is seriously overrated." Ingrid looked over at the Fiat. "I think you might need to adjust the carburetor a hair."

"What is this you're telling me?" Omar was bracing himself for more bad news.

"Forget what she said." I waved Ingrid's comment away. "My father broke up with Madame Godenot and begged my forgiveness at dinner and wants to get back together with my mother but now he's talking with Ingrid's dad and we don't know why but it looks kind of ominous because they were both in the war and you never know if—"

"My darling, please slow down. I don't know what you're saying," Omar pleaded, taking my hands.

"Wait. Here they come," Ingrid announced sotto voce.

Papi and Mr. Baum both looked a little shaken but rejoined us without saying a word.

"Hey, Dad. This is the boy I was telling you about. Omar Belhassine."

Omar stuck out his hand and gave my father a firm handshake, something I knew Papi respected as a sign of confident masculinity.

"Hmm," Papi said, giving him the once-over. He waited two seconds before relieving the tension. "So you're the lucky boy."

"I am indeed a lucky man," Omar said, smiling.

The correction from "boy" to "man" wasn't lost on Papi, and I could tell he appreciated it. *This fellow is solid*, I could hear him saying in Spanish. *Con este muchacho puedes contar.*

More introductions flew back and forth before Ingrid and

her father walked back along the gravel driveway to his car. They, too, were going out to dinner. Papi said he was exhausted from his travels and needed to return to his hotel room to rest. He flashed me a reassuring thumbs-up about Omar.

It wasn't until the next day that my father told me what'd happened with Mr. Baum. We were taking another walk along Lake Geneva and the ducks were squawking madly over some bread a decrepit man was flinging at them.

"He recognized me first," Papi said. "I'm not sure how. It's been almost thirty years. But as he began talking to me, I realized that he was the young officer I once knew."

"Did he do something bad to you?" I asked, afraid that he would tell me something so terrible that it might rupture my friendship with Ingrid.

"On the contrary, *mi amor*. He saved my life."

"What?!" I stopped in my tracks and stared up at him.

"I was supposed to be killed. This was right after the Warsaw ghetto uprising. I was involved in the resistance. I know I've told you part of this story."

"Only part?"

Papi motioned for me to be patient.

"As a teenager, I was a messenger for Mordecai Anielewicz, who'd led the revolt. I knew my way around the city and slipped through its back alleys like a ghost in the night. We'd organized and fought the Germans when they tried to round up another group for deportation. We held out for nearly a month. I've already described to you the suffering we endured. Ultimately, we were no match for the Nazis. They starved us, crushed us.

Then tens of thousands more were sent to the camps. I don't know how many were lined up to be shot."

Papi stopped, swallowing hard, and signaled for me to sit down next to him on a bench. Seagulls hovered over us, as if expecting us to toss them a few sardines. The boats on the lake looked motionless.

"Ingrid's father was an ordinary German soldier, if one could use such a benign term. What I mean to say is that he wasn't among those in charge. I don't know why or how he singled me out, but he did. On the pretext of marching me over to the local Nazi headquarters to extract more information, he spared my life. He could've chosen anyone on that line sentenced to death. But he chose me."

Papi looked down at his hands, as if they were somehow complicit in his survival, guilty for living when so many others had perished. I couldn't believe what he was telling me. How was I supposed to make sense of this? Ingrid's father saved my own father's life. The chain of events rattled in my head. The implications were more than I could fathom.

"He prodded me with his bayonet, forced me to clasp my hands behind my head as we marched through the rubble that was Warsaw. Everyone turned their heads as I passed, pretending I was invisible. When the German soldier ordered me behind a building, I thought he would shoot me on the spot. Instead he told me this: 'Run for your life, Jew.' Then he walked away without looking back."

"That was Ingrid's father?" I stammered. "Are you sure?"

"As sure as I stand here before you."

"Why didn't you ever tell us this? All those seders, all those stories you recounted about your escape?"

"I hadn't wanted to give credit to a German, *hija*. I hadn't wanted to believe there could be a single decent one." Papi breathed deeply as the last of the sun disappeared behind the distant Alps. "The rest of the story you know well from my telling. I ran for two years until I finally reached Cuba. And it was there, my dear Vivien, that my life truly began."

SHIRIN

I had not realized the power of silence, of withholding information until I had spent two days with my brother without telling him my dreadful secret. It felt as though there was a frozen mountain between us. Perhaps this was why he suggested we go to Paris for a brief escape. Cyrus rented a bright red Porsche roadster and threw our overnight bags in the minuscule trunk. What should have taken us six hours took us only three and a half. My brother drove the way he flew his fighter jets—breaking the sound barrier.

It had been many years since we had been to Paris together. Our parents had taken the family one April when I was five years old. I do not remember much about the trip except for the Cathedral of Notre Dame, and I only remember it because Cyrus had told me that this was where the fearsome hunchback lived. He teased me about the hunchback, threatening to invite him to dinner or on our chartered boat ride along the Seine. Once he stuffed the back of his shirt with a hotel pillow, encircled his eyes with my mother's dark lipstick, and, dragging one leg, scared me half out of my wits. How we laughed about this for years!

This trip was different, however. While the surface of our

conversations was lighthearted—Cyrus even tried the old hunchback trick on me again—it was impossible for me to keep my sorrow hidden completely. My brother must have sensed this because he gave me ample opportunity to unburden myself. *Tell me what's wrong, Shirin. What are you hiding?* In response, I would change the subject to something I knew would interest him.

We discussed the latest developments in mathematics and hotly debated the directions in the field. Cyrus spoke about the Air Force's next generation of jets. He complained that the shah was wasting billions on fancy equipment when the educational system was prehistoric. Gently, my brother also broke the news that my mother's beloved pet, a miniature poodle named Touki, had died of a stroke. This saddened me so much that I wept for an hour. Cyrus suspected that something else was causing my distress.

On our second day in Paris, my brother took me for a walk down its grand boulevards. We climbed the Eiffel Tower and joined the hordes of tourists at the Louvre. By late afternoon, we were tired and settled in the Luxembourg Gardens with pistachio ice cream cones (our favorite). The sky was cloudless and the air was redolent with tulips and jasmine, reminding me of our gardens back home. One boy in short pants chased a bigger version of himself over a stolen toy truck, to the dismay of their mother. As my brother crunched the last of his cone, he turned to me, one arm draped along the back of our bench, and looked at me with utmost seriousness.

"It's time for the truth, Shirin. No more secrets."

I began to cough and dropped my ice cream cone. I looked down at it and thought I might cry again. It took every bit of self-control I had to remain outwardly calm. Had my brother found out about my pregnancy? Could Vivien have betrayed my secret? Would Cyrus inform our parents? Would I ever be able to go home again? I thought all this in the split second before my brother continued.

"I have something to tell you. I've been wanting to tell you this for months but I didn't know how. Of course, I wanted to look you in the face when I did."

Slowly, I lifted my head and stared into his eyes. I needed to be stoic and honest with him. I would not deny what I had done. A flock of pigeons wheeled high above us, giving me courage.

"You, of all people, would understand how there are things you can't plan for in life. How sometimes things just happen, beyond one's control, as if preordained at birth," he said thoughtfully.

Perhaps he had rehearsed this speech for me. I feared what would come next, but he did not appear angry. Surprisingly, he seemed wary and solicitous.

"Do you understand, Shirin?"

"I think so," I mumbled.

"So then you know already?"

"Know what?" I asked, growing puzzled.

Cyrus took a deep breath. "That I am homosexual?"

My brain stopped for a minute as I blinked at him in confusion.

"I am in love with a man. His name is Mustafa and he is a pilot, like me." My brother's face softened with the memory of his beloved.

"You are in love?" I asked, disbelieving and relieved and

shocked simultaneously. Was it my imagination, or had every bird in the vicinity stopped chirping?

"Yes, Shirin." He scanned my face, trying to read my reaction.

I wasn't sure how I felt at that moment. Like a bolt, I realized that we were much more alike than different. That he, too, carried a secret; perhaps many secrets. That he was living a double life. I understood what it meant to hide oneself, to shield one's true life from the prying, judgmental eyes of others. The fact that he was my own brother, a member of the same family I feared disappointing, made the realization all the more potent.

And yet, I was upset and disturbed. The brother I thought I knew was someone else. A man who loved other men, who made love to other men. I imagined my parents' reaction. This would wound them much worse than if they had discovered my pregnancy. They must not find out about Cyrus, or me, or they would surely disown us. I was not sure I could tell him my secret even though he had just confided in me his darkest truth. Perhaps we would need to live in the shadows forever.

I looked up at Cyrus. He smiled at me but his eyes looked worried. They seemed to ask: Would I still love him? I asked this of myself and the answer helped clear the tangled roar in my brain. Yes, I loved my brother. Without a doubt, I loved him. Unequivocally. This would never change.

"Are you happy?" I managed to ask.

He nodded, still searching my eyes for a response.

"Then I am happy for you, dear Cyrus." I leaned toward him and embraced him with all the strength in my arms.

DAY
TWENTY-SEVEN

INGRID

So how crazy was that? It turned out that my father was a fucking war hero. Let me rephrase that. Vati did one thing that was heroic—and it so happened to be saving the life of my best friend's dad. It blew my mind to think about it. What were the odds of this? Like one in seventeen trillion? The fact is, Vivien wouldn't exist if it hadn't been for my father. It made me feel like her destiny and mine were intertwined somehow, inextricably so; that we were meant to be friends because of what'd happened long ago. The craziest part was that Vati had no idea about the fate of the man he'd pulled off the line to be shot in Warsaw thirty years earlier. As far as he knew, the guy might've been killed ten minutes after he'd set him free.

Trust me when I say that this news coming to light didn't alleviate my father's horrendous guilt over the war. He'd done a lot of things that he claimed would torment him for the rest of his days. I heard some of his stories at the front gates of Dachau and on our way home from Germany. Vati told me that he was just a kid when his parents forced him to drop out of high school and take a job as a guard at the concentration camp—to help with the family's finances. His father had lost a leg in World War I and hadn't held a steady job since. Plus he drank a lot and beat up on his family when he did. Not a great legacy, to say the least.

Anyway, Vati told me that working at Dachau was the beginning of his ten-year career with the Nazis. He admitted that he'd followed orders that whole atrocious decade except for the one incomprehensible act of compassion that saved Max Wahl's life in 1944. If I wrote this in a book, nobody would believe me.

It made me start thinking of bigger things, cosmic coincidences, the possibility of a God, the poetics of an inexplicable universe. Was this simply an astounding but meaningless fluke that would never be repeated in the history of mankind? Or were Vivien and I supposed to somehow close a karmic circle?

In the wake of this revelation, my petty obsessions subsided drastically. Sure, I wanted to get my photographs back but I didn't need to ruin Gerhardt in the process. He hadn't forced me to sleep with him. If anything, I was the one who'd come on to him. I was kidding myself by trying to entrap him on corrupting-a-minor charges. Really, I had better things to do with my time. Like picking up a goddamn camera and taking more pictures, for starters. Nobody was stopping me except myself. If my father was capable of such an incredible act of heroism, why couldn't I soar above the crap and move on with my own life?

The Friday before summer session ended at Pierpont, Vati and Mr. Wahl went out to lunch. I never found out what they talked about those five hours they were huddled over their steaks and *pommes frites*. No amount of haranguing pried information loose from either of them. All I learned was that when they returned from lunch that afternoon, their ties loosened, their faces flushed with too much wine, they'd become, if not friends, then something equally profound. Something forged of gratitude and relief, pain and forgiveness. Maybe even a measure of delight in whom the other had become.

DAYS
TWENTY-EIGHT
&
TWENTY-NINE

VIVIEN

It wouldn't be an exaggeration to say that I never worked so hard in my life as I did those two days of cooking madness in Lausanne. Thirty young chefs from around Europe gathered in the vast kitchens of the city's oldest, most elegant hotel to battle for the title of Chef de l'Avenir and a full scholarship to Le Cordon Bleu cooking school in Paris. Our mission was to whip up three dishes in four categories: appetizers, entrées, side dishes, and desserts. The judges would evaluate us on each category as well as the "conceptual progression" of the menu.

After slaving away all summer on dozens of far-flung recipes,

I had a major brainstorm. I had decided that for each category I would prepare something Cuban, something Iranian, and something German—in honor of my friendships with Shirin and Ingrid. For me, this meant a couple of demented all-nighters mastering new techniques. But I was determined to pull it off.

Each contestant was given two sous chefs to work with. I jettisoned mine after they rolled their eyes at the mere mention of what I was planning. With the fierce intervention of Madame Sarazin, I was allowed to take on Cyrus and Ingrid as my assistants. They defrocked their predecessors of their aprons and toques, rolled up their sleeves, and cooked side-by-side with me every step of the way. It would've been difficult for me to conjure up those rhapsodic Persian dishes without Cyrus, who turned out to be a superb chef in his own right. And Ingrid was positively uncompromising over her German dishes. She wielded a knife with impressive finesse, too, which came in handy chopping mounds of onions and fending off a saboteur from the Italian team.

My father, Omar, Shirin, Madame Sarazin, and a vocal coterie of supporters from Pierpont kept us going through the grueling competition. I was the youngest contestant there and considered by many to be the underdog. This made me a crowd favorite, especially against the snooty Parisian chefs. After the first day of competition, I was interviewed for the evening news. I caused a scandal by insisting that cultural fusions of every kind were happening all over the globe— except in Old World kitchens.

Anyway, here's what we presented, mixed and inventively matched into three, original, cross-cultural menus:

APPETIZERS:

yucca in garlic sauce (Cuban)

zwiebelküchen (German onion pie)

dolmeh

(Persian grape leaves stuffed with spiced ground lamb)

ENTRÉES:

ropa vieja (my Tía Cuca's famous flank steak stew)

pork chops with sauerkraut (a Baum family favorite)

khoresht fesenjan

(chicken in pomegranate and walnut sauce)

SIDE DISHES:

frijoles negros

(Cuban black beans served over fluffy white rice)

spätzle (traditional German dumplings)

kashk-e bademjan

(fried eggplant with yogurt and mint)

DESSERTS:

mango flan (just thinking about it makes me salivate)

German apple cake

Persian ice cream with rose water and pistachios

The judges commented that they were impressed by my team's variety of unusual offerings. Unfortunately, they did *not* concur that combining the cuisines of such radically different culinary traditions proved to be, as one chef proclaimed in his closing remarks, "an entirely joyful union." So much for cross-cultural cooperation.

But our chicken in pomegranate and walnut sauce came in third place among the entrées, after a savory bouillabaisse and a perfectly cooked rack of lamb (basically, the same old French classics). Ingrid was muttering about how the award should be called Chef du Passé instead of Chef de l'Avenir, and I had to grind my heel into her foot to keep her from going off on the judges altogether. My mango flan also won a respectable fifth place among the tantalizing desserts. The German dishes, to Ingrid's disgust, all came in last. She chalked it up to historical rivalries beyond her control.

Okay, so I didn't win the competition, or the full scholarship to cooking school, or heap any more glory on Pierpont's already storied reputation. (In fact, the only thing I won was a set of decent kitchen knives as a consolation prize for the Persian chicken dish.) But no matter what the judges decided, I learned that I could take the heat and pressure of a world-class kitchen, and survive.

When Shirin, Ingrid, and I clasped one another in our own victory circle in the middle of that swanky hotel kitchen in Lausanne, laughing and crying and making impossible promises to each other, I believed the feeling would never end. We hugged so hard and so long that we knew we'd stay together no matter how far afield we went. If you'd asked any of us where our dreams might take us, our answers wouldn't have been as certain as knowing, in our hearts, that our friendship would last forever.

EPILOGUE

1983

SHIRIN

It is hard to believe that a decade has passed since our last fateful summer together. I returned to Iran to finish my studies, completing a double doctorate in physics and mathematics (the first woman in my country's history to do so). When the revolution triumphed, all my family—except for my father and me—fled to Europe. I have not seen any of them in four years. They wanted no part of the ayatollah's fundamentalist government. My mother lives in London. Cyrus lives in the south of France with his new lover, a cruise ship captain (nobody in my family will acknowledge that he is gay), and my other brothers settled in Germany with their families. Only Baba and I remained behind, in a mansion that is crumbling, with only one last loyal servant to care for us.

I married and quickly divorced a fellow mathematician, who then emigrated to Sweden and now teaches at a second-rate university in Stockholm. His only parting gift to me was the seed he implanted in my womb, that of my precious daughter, whom I named Vivien Ingrid Firouz. My father and I are raising her together amidst the detritus of war-torn Tehran. I can assure you that despite our troubling circumstances, no child in the world is more loved. Little Vivi is nearly four years old. Already she is reading well and extrapolating numbers with great success. I suspect she will follow in my footsteps. After the revolution I was forbidden to teach at the university and placed in an all-girls elementary school instead. It is not what I expected to do, but I consider it noble work to shape the minds of the next generation of women.

Ingrid managed to see me when I was eight-and-a-half months pregnant, fat and blooming with life. She had come to Iran to cover the early days of the revolution for an international news magazine. That was what she did then and, I presume, to this day. She showed up at my father's house one morning wearing sunglasses, khaki fatigues, and draped with cameras, her pockets stuffed with film. Ingrid had given up the world of fine art, with its dazzling openings and wealthy patrons, to bring to light the ravages of war, revolution, famine, genocide, injustice. This was her calling now and she was good at it, famous for it, even more so than she had been for her photographs of Arabian stallions and pubescent girls.

I was so pleased to see her that I cried with happiness. Ingrid was in Tehran for a week and we got together nearly every day. I do not know whether it was the excitement of her visits or the ferocity and uncertainty of the revolution, but

I went into early labor. There were complications and I was put under general anesthesia, at the direction of my father. When I woke up, Baba handed me my daughter, beautiful and alert and healthy. That day—and it was the last day I ever saw Ingrid—she visited me in the hospital with a bouquet of yellow tulips. She took pictures of my baby girl but I never saw the photographs she had promised me.

It has been many more years since I have seen dear Vivien. We arranged to meet in Rome in the spring of 1977, when she was doing a practicum at an Italian restaurant on the outskirts of the capital. She was as plump and optimistic as I had ever seen her. She swore she was in love with a Polish chef back in New York. How we laughed at the culinary possibilities of that match! We continued to write to each other until the revolution made our correspondence impossible. Ingrid swore that she would tell Vivien about my daughter, that I had named her, lovingly, after the two of them, my dearest friends in the world. But I have heard nothing from either one these last years. It is this hope—to learn news of them—along with the daily delight of my daughter, the precious light of my life, that keeps me going day after day.

INGRID

What can I say about my life? If I had sum it up in one word, it would be *unhinged*, seriously unhinged. Basically, I live on planes, running from one disaster to another, from one adrenaline rush to the next. That's what photojournalists do. Most people, even hardened war correspondents, hear an explosion and hit the floor in self-defense, or run for their lives. Photojournalists run *toward* the blast. It's counter-intuitive and dangerous, but that's how we live.

At this point in my life, I wouldn't know how else to be. My work is what defines me. When I see my photographs on the cover of *Paris Match* or the front page of the *New York Times*, I know I've done my job. It's not the being there, the documenting of war and horror that's important, but conveying it to the rest of the world—making it a matter of crucial importance to everyone sitting cozily in their living rooms, far from the danger. I look at what nobody wants to look at, hold my gaze steady, aim my camera, and then stop time.

Those summers in Switzerland taught me a lot about what I *didn't* wanted to do. I didn't want to grow up and live off my parents, or a husband, or the rich snobs who could make or break my career as a fine-arts photographer. I wanted to do something that had the potential to change lives—or, if not change them, then at least record them in a way that made it impossible for anyone to ignore. I wanted people who saw my photographs to feel a crushing sense of complicity for doing nothing.

This year alone, I've covered the aftermath of the bombing of the American embassy in Beirut. Three days later, I was photographing the U.S. invasion of Grenada. Over the summer, I crisscrossed the Philippines documenting the unrest that followed the assassination of Benigno Aquino. Last year was insane, too: the Israeli invasion of Lebanon; the outlandish Falklands war. Recently I've begun a photo essay on an insidious, deadly new disease that's spreading in the gay community and in Africa. People are terrified of it. Nobody knows how it's transmitted, though everyone suspects it's sexual. Researchers say it could turn into a pandemic, claim millions of lives.

None of this leaves me much time for a personal life. I grab my pleasures wherever and whenever I can. Sometimes I don't even know their names. Once in a blue moon, when I stop long enough to think about it, I get depressed, at least until the next assignment puts me in high gear. It's a privilege, really, to live as I do. I get to look death straight in the eye nearly every single day. Strange as it sounds, its proximity makes me live all the harder.

Now and then I see Vivien in New York. She's opened a tiny restaurant on the Lower East Side amidst the punk rockers and Ukrainian cafeterias. Her place is a wacky combination of Cuban and Polish cuisine, a tribute to her heritage and to Eliasz, the man she's living with. He's this big bear of a guy who escaped the Iron Curtain and made his way first to Berlin, then Paris, then to cooking school in New York, where they met. They're pretty fat and happy together but it's not a life I could ever choose.

Sometimes Vivien and I meet late at night for drinks. Over a couple of bottles of wine, we reminisce about our summers in Switzerland. I swear she's an eternal optimist because she remembers only the good times: sunset rides on the Arabian stallions; Omar's long and florid courtship of her; our solidarity during that cooking contest in Lausanne. Maybe it's the way I'm wired, but I tend to remember entirely different things, hurtful things that have left their mark. I guess that's why Vivien offers up love and food to her customers every day, whereas it's my business to present the harsher realities of life.

We talk a lot about Shirin when we get together. We wonder how her life is turning out in Tehran, how she's surviving the brutal war with Iraq. She's the only one of us who has a child. Her daughter means the world to her. But this devotion keeps Shirin stuck in one place. After that first bottle of wine, Vivien and I vow to figure out a way to visit her, although we both know, deep down, that this is highly unlikely. No foreign journalists are allowed in Iran anymore, and the place is sealed shut from outsiders. Still, we dream of surprising Shirin in her father's house, bringing toys for her daughter. Who might she become with a name like Vivien Ingrid Firouz? I, for one, want to survive long enough to find out.

VIVIEN

I had big dreams when I was younger, much bigger than I ended up needing them to be. I wanted to be a world-famous chef. I wanted my parents to get back together and live happily ever after. I wanted Omar's family to fall in love with me, even though I was from the other side of the world and ill-suited to be an ambitious politician's wife. Of course, none of this happened.

I'm a good chef. Some people would argue that I'm a great chef, and I wouldn't dispute this. But the world-famous part ceased to be very important to me after a while. My little twenty-two-seat restaurant is perfect for me and my boyfriend, Eliasz. We dish up only what pleases us to eat. Officially, we mix up Cuban ham croquettes with Polish pierogis, but unofficially, the menu varies wildly from day to day. It's an insane amount of work but lots of fun. Plus I'm madly in love.

As for my parents, they finally did remarry. But their marriage barely lasted another year. I felt guilty for wishing for something that proved so wrong and painful for both of them. My mother married again this past winter. I like her husband—a veterinarian who specializes in exotic pets and dabbles in dinner theater on the side. I don't really consider him family, though. Papi, heartbroken, recently relocated to South Africa to be closer to his diamond mines. My grandmother and Tía Cuca both died a few years ago, so I have nobody left who can point to me and say *I saw her do that when she was five.*

As for Omar and me, we dated longer than anyone might've imagined. I even went to visit him in Tunisia, where my reception was chilly at best. In the end, it came down to religion. I didn't feel strongly enough about either Catholicism or Islam to make that kind of commitment. Omar wanted to follow his father into politics and he needed a traditional wife. Obviously, I didn't fit the bill. I'll always be grateful to him for that long stretch of adoration he bestowed on me. Omar was the first boy I made love with, and he set the standard for both the gentleness and ardor I treasure in my boyfriend today.

I wish I could say that Ingrid, Shirin, and I have stayed best friends forever. But it's been six years since I saw Shirin in Italy and so much has happened to us both. It's sad that we can't write to each other because of the war and the U.S. blockade against Iran. It's like Cuba all over again. Ingrid, unsurprisingly, is a perennial globetrotter, restless and curious as ever. A part of me lives through her adventures—from the comfort of my kitchen. If we're lucky, we get to see each other once or twice a year.

At least this much I can say is still true: Nobody I've met, nor anything I've done in the last ten years, has come close to the intensity that Ingrid, Shirin, and I experienced those three unforgettable summers in Switzerland. We may not be in constant touch, or know the minute details of one another's days, but I know that what my heart wants is what their hearts want, too: to know that our friendship matters deeply, significantly, and that what we once lived and learned from one another, nobody can take away.

  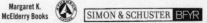

Road Trip Checklist

- a brother's dying wish
- his cocky best friend
- a beat-up Chevy Impala
- one pair of red cowboy boots